MY
Destiny

MY Destiny

ESSENCE BESTSELLING AUTHOR

ADRIANNE BYRD

HARLEQUIN®

entertain, enrich, inspire™

Recycling programs
for this product may
not exist in your area.

MY DESTINY

ISBN-13: 978-0-373-53489-0

Copyright © 2003 by Adrianne Byrd

First published by BET Publications, LLC in 2003.

This book is dedicated in loving memory to
Robert Saulsbery.
It was nice to finally meet you…and love you.

In the Beginning...

Chapter 1

Destiny Brockman cursed a blue streak as she struggled out of the elevator with a box that was twice her size. Her arms burned and a painful cramp crept along her back.

"It's just a little farther," she encouraged herself in a shaky whisper. In the back of her mind she wondered: Where on earth was Lu Jin? She was supposed to be helping her.

She heard a sudden rush of footsteps, but before she knew what happened, she smacked into something hard and nearly lost her grip on the box.

"Damn, man," a male voice roared. "Why don't you look where you're going?"

"I'm doing the best I can," she snapped back. She shook her head and flipped a few errant strands of hair from her eyes so she could see who she'd bumped into.

Destiny's knees buckled at the unexpected vision of a gorgeous brother with strong chiseled features and skin the color of milk chocolate.

When his full lips widened, she experienced a strange flutter in her chest. His hair was a low, barely-there buzz cut which gave him a clean look, but it was his devilish hazel eyes framed by long, curly lashes that threatened to steal her heart. No man should have such beautiful eyes.

"Well, well. Where are my manners?" the man said in a sexy baritone that could make a nun blush. "The name's Miles Stafford."

Destiny gave her head a firm shake and broke the strange hypnotic spell she'd fallen under. "Hello. Excuse me." She stepped around him.

He quickly blocked her passage again. "I...uh, live in apartment fourteen twenty-seven."

"Congratulations," she said, cynically.

Miles laughed; it was a boisterous, husky vibrato that was as sexy as it was infectious. "My, what a sharp tongue you have. How intriguing." He winked.

She felt, as well as watched, his gaze roam over her again and that strange fluttering returned. "I'm sorry, but if you don't mind, I need to set this box down before my arms snap off."

"Oh, here. Let me help you with that." With what seemed like little effort, Miles took possession of the box as if it weighed nothing. "Just lead the way."

Although thankful, Destiny grudgingly rewarded him with a tight smile. She stepped around him again and as she led him to apartment fourteen twenty-six, she noticed for the first time the man's enormous size. He was an easy six-foot-four with broad shoulders and a narrow waist. His cologne tickled her nose and it took all she had not to lose herself in its light mixtures of musk and...well, she couldn't place her finger on it, but damn he smelled good.

"Don't tell me we're going to be neighbors," Miles said when she reached for her doorknob.

Destiny nodded. "Sort of looks that way." She wanted to hurry. The sooner he set the box down, the sooner he'd leave. Pushing open the door, they were immediately greeted with the sight of Lu Jin, her beautiful Black-Asian friend, laughing on the phone. The laughter stopped when Lu Jin turned toward them.

"Hello," Miles said.

"Monique, let me call you back. Someone has just popped in." Lu Jin ended the call without further explanation, and then turned her Hollywood smile on her friend. "Well, hello to you, too." She cast Destiny a curious look.

Destiny shrugged, then turned back toward her new neighbor. "Thanks for bringing that in for me. My friend here had disappeared, apparently taking an important phone call," she added with mild sarcasm. "You can set it down right there."

Miles turned and did as he was instructed. When he stood erect again, the entire apartment seemed to shrink around them. The man was gorgeous, no ifs, ands or buts about it. When he smiled at them, he showed two perfect rows of straight, white teeth.

Lu Jin navigated her slender body between Destiny and Miles and extended her hand in greeting. "My name is Lu Jin."

"Miles Stafford."

"A handsome name for a handsome man," Lu Jin said.

Destiny rolled her eyes heavenward at Lu Jin's flirting. She watched as he took her friend's hand and lifted it to his lips, but it was Destiny he winked at as he kissed Lu Jin's hand.

Destiny dropped her gaze.

"Handsome as well as chivalrous. Tell your girlfriend I'm jealous," Lu Jin baited coolly.

His rich laughter encircled the women. "I don't have a steady girl right now." He waited until he caught Destiny's gaze again. "But I'm looking."

Destiny's smile tightened as she stepped around her friend. "Well, we wouldn't want to keep you from your vigilant search."

Miles's brows rose with amusement. He followed her to the door. "Beautiful, and with a wicked sense of humor. Tell your man that I'm jealous."

Lu Jin spoke up. "Destiny doesn't—"

"I'll make sure I do that," Destiny drowned out her friend and held open the door and waited until he crossed the threshold. "Thank you again for helping me with the box."

"Destiny, eh?" He lifted an inquisitive brow while another sly smile slid into place. "Interesting name for an interesting woman."

Something about the man's cockiness continued to rub Destiny the wrong way. "Again, thanks." She forced an amicable smile and hoped it didn't look as plastic as it felt.

"Hey, that's what neighbors are for, right? Maybe one day I can ask you to do me a favor."

Destiny frowned, and then opened her mouth to respond when a syrupy-sweet feminine voice floated toward them.

"Oh, there you are, Miles."

Destiny and Miles turned.

The first thing Destiny noticed was the woman's incredible legs. They were long, toned and seemed to go on forever. Next were the woman's breasts—perfect circular orbs that seemed to be oblivious to gravity. They couldn't possibly be real, Destiny thought critically.

"You naughty boy," the woman cooed as she looped a protective arm through Miles's. "When I turned around at the party you were gone. I didn't know where you'd run off to until Wes said he thought you ran to your apartment to get something." She turned her bright smile toward Destiny. "Who's your new friend?"

Destiny, who was still scrutinizing the leggy woman, crossed her arms. "We're hardly friends."

Miles's smile grew wider. "True, but one never knows what the future holds."

"Well, my name is Celeste Silverman." She thrust out her hand.

"Destiny Brockman."

They shook hands while Destiny looked over at Miles.

There was that damn smile of his again. He could have at least had the courtesy to look embarrassed for having a half-dressed hussy draped around him, but instead he looked perfectly at ease.

"Thanks again for your help." She cast Celeste another glance, and then shut the door.

Destiny turned and rolled her eyes heavenward.

Lu Jin fanned herself with her hands. "Now that brother is *fine*. Are you sure that I can't convince you to take me on as a roommate?"

"Please. We can do a lot better than become another notch on that man's bedpost."

Lu Jin laughed. "Whatever, girl. I'm not the least bit surprised that women are coming out of the woodwork for him. Did you get a good look at him? Jeez, I think I need a drink. Do you have anything in this place?"

"Sorry. Stocking the bar wasn't high on my priority list today. Besides," Destiny said, stomping past her, "aren't you suppose to be helping me with this move?"

"I am helping. I've already unpacked a box of dishes in the kitchen."

"That was over an hour ago."

"I had to take a phone call, slave-driver. Besides, I thought you said Elliott and Zack were supposed to be helping."

Destiny frowned and glanced at her watch. "Yeah, they should have been here by now."

Lu Jin extracted a box cutter from the back pocket of her jeans and slit open a nearby box marked LINENS.

"Frankly, I hate that Elliott didn't get a chance to see Mr. Fine checking you out. I think it's just the push he needs to make his move on you before someone else snatches you up."

"What are you talking about?"

"Come on, girl. Everyone knows he has the hots for you. Everyone, that is, except for you."

Destiny reached inside the linen box and removed a stack of pink bath towels. "Elliott and I are just friends. That's all."

"And why is that?" Lu Jin jabbed her fist against her hips. "Because you are too stuck up for your own good."

"What?" Destiny exclaimed with an incredulous half laugh.

"You heard me. I'm only telling you this because I'm your friend."

Destiny frowned. "With friends like you—"

"Yeah, yeah, whatever. Look, I'm telling you that you need to loosen up. Get your nose out of your law books and have a little fun."

"I have plenty of fun."

"Oh, yeah? When? I can't remember the last time you went out on a date."

"There are other important things in life besides dating, you know."

Lu Jin rolled her eyes. "I don't want to hear another long soliloquy about how important your job is again. I swear I'll barf right here on your new rug."

Destiny's eyes narrowed. "You know, you can be an ass at times. I never made fun of your aspirations to be some grand Broadway actress, especially since you've never even been within a hundred miles of New York."

Lu Jin held up her hands. "You're right. I'm sorry." When Destiny didn't respond, she draped an arm around Destiny's shoulders and pulled her close. "Come on. Who loves ya, baby?"

"Well, we hate to interrupt you two lovebirds." A male voice chuckled and penetrated the women's private sanctuary.

The two women jumped and turned to face three men standing at the front door: Elliott, Zack and Miles.

Zack, a long-time friend of both girls snickered as he moved farther into the room. "Too bad we didn't bring our video camera. Sounds like we interrupted the makings of a good adult film."

Lu Jin shot Zack the bird and directed him to "Go to hell."

"I just came back for this," Miles said, stooping over to pick up a watch near the box he'd delivered. "It must have come off earlier." He glanced at Destiny and allowed his gaze to swing between her and Lu Jin.

"Well, what can I say," Lu Jin swung her arm back around Destiny and joined Zack in his little joke. "Destiny is the only woman for me."

Destiny's eyes rounded as her mouth dropped open.

"I better get going," Miles said, and then turned back toward the men he'd entered with. "It was nice meeting you two."

Elliott nodded as joyful tears glistened in his eyes. "It was nice meeting you, too." He shook Miles's hand.

Miles smiled and rushed to slip out the front door.

Destiny's friends roared with laughter.

"I can't believe you guys just did that," she said. "He probably believed y'all."

Lu Jin trembled with mirth as she dropped onto the couch.

Destiny grabbed one of the throw pillows and smacked her, which only seemed to further tickle her friend.

"I'm serious."

Zack and Elliott joined Lu Jin on the couch. None of them

looking too concerned about the joke they'd embellished in front of Destiny's new neighbor and at her expense.

"I don't see what the big deal is." Lu Jin wiped at the corners of her eyes. "You just said a few minutes ago that you didn't like the man. So what difference does it make if he thinks you and I are an item?"

Destiny opened her mouth, but didn't have an answer.

Her friends laughed.

"See?" Lu Jin said, triumphantly. "It's no big deal—unless, of course, you were attracted to tall, dark and handsome."

Elliott's smile vanished.

"Of course not," Destiny answered.

"Good. Looks like we just did you a favor." Lu Jin jumped back to her feet and slapped her hands together. "Let's get back to work. Now that the whole gang is here, we should be finished in no time."

Elliott jumped up. "Zack and I will bring up the boxes while you two unpack."

"Sounds like a plan to me." Destiny smiled, but couldn't help picturing the shock on Miles's face before he'd left—or had it been a flicker of disappointment?

Delicate fingers snapped in front of Miles's face and jarred him back to Celeste's beautiful face. They had returned to Wes's party. The large condo was packed with wall-to-wall people. The music was good, the food was wonderful and everyone was having a great time, which was the norm for Wes's infamous parties.

Celeste inched closer to Miles. "How come I get the feeling that dreamy expression on your face has nothing to do with me?"

Miles slid an arm around her small waist and whispered against her ear. "I wouldn't be too sure about that if I were you."

Her face glowed with anticipation as she stared up at him and he knew her next question long before she gave voice to it.

"How about we cut out of here early and go back to your place?" She rubbed against him for dramatic emphasis.

Miles lowered his gaze and was pretending to mull the proposition over when a heavy hand slapped him hard on the back.

"Everybody having a good time?" Wes Cunningham squeezed in between Miles and Celeste and draped his arms around their shoulders.

Miles took one look at Wes's glossy eyes and knew that his best friend was drunk.

"Celeste, Celeste," Wes murmured as he looked her over. "When are you going to come to your senses and realize that I'm the man of your dreams?"

She laughed and pinched his dimpled cheek. "To quote a good friend of mine, 'You never know what the future holds.'" She glanced over at Miles and caught his amused expression.

Wes pounded Miles's back. "Better watch out, bro. I'm giving serious thoughts to stealing this one from you."

Miles laughed. "You can't steal what I don't possess."

Celeste's smile slipped.

"Or someone who doesn't want to be possessed," he added smoothly, before taking a deep sip of his wine.

A woman with more curves than any man would know what to do with passed before the trio and both men watched the seductive sway of her hips.

Celeste cleared her throat and regained the men's attention.

Wes smiled while Miles refused to appear contrite.

"Do you hear that, Sweetheart?" Wes's arm fell from Miles's shoulders to pull Celeste closer to him. "It sounds like you're a free agent."

"So it would seem," she said, tightly. Her malevolent gaze leveled with Miles.

"Aw, come on." Wes draped his arm back around Miles to include him. "You know I was just playing with you guys. Loosen up. This is supposed to be a party."

Celeste shook her head. "I think I need some fresh air." In a flash, she slipped from under Wes's arm and disappeared into the crowd before either man had a chance to stop her.

"I take it she's upset," Wes said.

Miles shrugged. He wasn't in the mood to play head games with Celeste. "I'm sure she'll get over it."

Wes laughed and shook his head. "I don't get it. Women constantly throw themselves at you and you act like you don't notice or you don't care."

"There's an old saying—the one who cares the least in a relationship is the one who's in control of it."

Wes's eyes widened as if he'd just been enlightened. "I'll make sure that I remember that."

"Besides, life's too short for a bunch of drama," Miles murmured.

"Come on, man. You're still on that kick that you're going to die young?"

The light buzz Miles had been enjoying from his wine vanished. "This is not just some overblown superstition, Wes. I come from a long line of men who never live to see their forty-sixth birthday." He held Wes's gaze for a tense moment and then smiled in an effort to revive their earlier joviality. "Which is why I intend to live my life to the fullest. I'm going to drink, be merry and enjoy women."

Wes shrugged. "Best to go out with a smile, I always say."

Miles held up his glass in salute. "I'll drink to that."

"So you want to head on upstairs? I got a few dancers on the pole tonight. I guarantee they have what it takes to get your mind off Celeste for the rest of the night."

"Trust me. My head isn't stuck on Celeste."

"Oh, no?"

"Nah. Did you know that we have a new neighbor moving into the place across from here?"

"Oh, really? Male or female?"

"Female."

"Is she hot?"

"I thought so—until I met her girlfriend."

"Then why in the hell didn't you invite them to the party?"

"No, you don't understand. I mean her *girlfriend*."

Wes paused. "You mean…?"

"Yeah."

"Then you definitely should have invited them over. You know I'm down for a ménage à trois. Talk about getting your freak on. Is the girlfriend hot, too?"

Miles laughed good-naturedly. "They're both beautiful."

"Well, hell. I'll go and invite them." Wes turned and headed toward the door. He'd actually managed to maneuver through a few people before Miles caught up with him.

"I don't think that is such a good idea," Miles said, shaking his head and draping his arm around Wes's shoulders.

"Why not?"

"They don't strike me as the party type."

Wes frowned. "Well, what type are they?"

"Let it go. I'll find out the 4-1-1 on them soon enough. I think one of them may swing the other way."

"How do you know that?"

"She was flirting with me."

"No lie?" Wes's eyes lit with excitement, then quickly narrowed with suspicion. "How come I get the feeling that you don't want me to go over there because you're going to try and make a play for both of them?"

Miles laughed and lifted his wineglass in a mock toast. "Like I said, I plan to live life to the fullest."

Chapter 2

Lu Jin slashed open a box label CDS only to discover that it had been marked wrong. At first glance, she assumed the papers to be more of Destiny's legal briefs, but a newspaper heading caught and held her attention. She reached inside and withdrew a stack of newspaper clippings.

"Mystery Surrounds Attorney Adam Brockman's Suicide." Lu Jin flipped to another. "Sex, Lies and Political Favors Swirl Around Brockman's Untimely Death."

"What are you doing?" Destiny asked suddenly from behind her.

"Oh." Lu Jin jumped and dropped the clippings before looking guiltily at her best friend. "The box was labeled wrong," she confessed.

Destiny's gaze fell to the floor, but she didn't kneel to pick up the articles. "I knew I should have thrown those damn things away."

The weight of Lu Jin's stare finally forced Destiny to look back at her friend. "I'm hungry. You want to order a pizza?"

Lu Jin frowned, and then crossed her arms. "Why would you want to throw these away?"

Destiny shrugged and forced any telltale emotion from her voice. "Because it's been two years and it's time to move on."

Lu Jin held Destiny's gaze and then made a grand show of applauding. "Bravo. I think I'm not the only one who should be pursuing an acting career. Any way I can convince you to go to Broadway with me?"

Destiny rolled her eyes and knelt to pick up her belongings.

Lu Jin helped. "Are you still angry at Adam?"

"And if I told you that I wasn't?"

"I'd tell you your nose was growing."

"You're suppose to be my friend, not my therapist."

"You're right." Lu Jin nodded while thinking. "You should be paying me."

Destiny laughed and the tension dissipated. "I couldn't afford you anyway."

"You're probably right. As screwed up as you are I could wipe out your inheritance. Then maybe *I* could afford to live in this place."

Destiny continued laughing. When the joviality died, she looked at her best friend with sober eyes and confessed, "I miss him."

Lu Jin opened her arms and Destiny eased into her embrace.

Adam Brockman had been a hero to many people throughout his short life: whether it was during his time as the captain of the football team or later when he'd graduated cum laude from Princeton. He became a young trailblazer in the political world. Through it all, no one looked up to Adam Brockman more than his twin sister, Destiny.

Adam's suicide, as well as the rumored political corruption

that surrounded him, devastated young Destiny. So much so that at one point Destiny questioned her own ability to be a good lawyer. The news of her brother's failings also haunted her father, the Honorable Edward Brockman.

Her father spent his last days in shame of the scandal. When he passed away, it became an unspoken rule between Destiny and her mother not to speak of Adam, but every once in a while her brother's image crept into her dreams and she would wake to find her pillow soaked with tears.

Yet, somehow the corruption that followed Adam to his grave fed Destiny's resolve to redeem the Brockman name. She would succeed where her brother had failed.

There were times when she thought it ironic that she had once wanted to be like her brother and now she wanted to be better than him; sometimes that meant she needed to bury his memory. However, there was a part of her that wouldn't allow her to do that, it was the part that wouldn't allow her to throw away the newspaper clippings.

"You know a pizza does sound good," Lu Jin said almost wistfully.

Destiny pulled out of Lu Jin's arms. "Sounds wonderful. Let's ask the guys."

"I will if they ever get back up here. They went down for more boxes, I swear, half an hour ago."

Destiny frowned. "You don't think they dipped on us?"

"I'll kill them."

"It would be just like them to show up late and leave early."

"It's hard to find good help." Lu Jin got to her feet. "So what'll ya have? Meat Lovers or Supreme?"

Destiny's stomach growled as if it were trying to answer for her.

Lu Jin and Destiny laughed.

"Let's go with the Meat Lovers and make it a large," Destiny said.

"You got it." Lu Jin went in search of the cordless phone.

Destiny smiled as she watched her. She couldn't have asked for a better friend than Lu Jin. Of this, she was sure. They'd met in their freshman year at college—an awkward time in both of their lives. The two roommates couldn't have been more different, but somehow they'd managed to create a bond that each cherished.

Zack and Elliott breezed into the apartment. Neither carried a box.

Destiny and Lu Jin rushed into the living room and simultaneously crossed their arms while Destiny demanded, "Where have you two been?"

Zack eased forward with a wide smile. "There's one heck of a party at the condo on the other side of the building. You girls need to come and check it out."

"You've been at a party all this time?" Destiny asked. "I thought you two were supposed to be helping me?"

"We are—we will. I mean—you've got to come and check out this party."

"I'm not about to crash some party and I can't believe you guys have. These people are going to be my neighbors, remember? What if they find out you two weren't invited?"

"Hey, we *were* invited. Some guy in the elevator told us we needed to check it out," Elliott defended and moved to stand next to Zack. "Take my word for it, you ain't never seen a party like this. There's something for everyone."

"Oh?" Lu Jin perked with interest.

"That's just great. I take it you're going to bail out on me, as well?"

"No." She looked to the guys. "I mean, uh…"

"All we're suggesting is that we take an hour break, socialize with your new neighbors, then resume working. That's all," Elliott said.

"You two just got here about an hour ago and now your need a break?"

Lu Jin draped her arm around Destiny's shoulder. "Now, calm down. There's no need for you to get upset. We promised you that we'd help and that's what we're going to do. Right, guys?"

Crestfallen, the guys nodded.

"Even if it takes all weekend," Lu Jin continued. "We're just asking for an hour break—which we were about to take anyway once we ordered a pizza."

Destiny suddenly felt as though she was being the bad guy by forcing her friends into doing something they apparently didn't feel like doing.

"Fine. Go to the party. I don't care." She turned away from them.

Zack and Elliott raced toward the door, hoping to escape before Destiny changed her mind.

"Why don't you come with us?" Lu Jin suggested.

Destiny shook her head. "That's all right. You go ahead on. I'll see you back here in an hour."

Lu Jin didn't immediately head for the door. "Are you sure?"

Destiny faced her. "I'm sure. Go have fun. It's okay."

Lu Jin still didn't move.

"You better hurry up. Your hour is going to be over soon."

"All right."

Destiny waited until Lu Jin closed the door behind her before she slumped to the floor in defeat. Why did she always have to come off acting like a prude? So what if her friends wanted to go hang out at some party?

"Nice going, Destiny," she mumbled. There were times when she envied Lu Jin and her spontaneity. Whereas Destiny was reclusive, Lu Jin was gregarious. People had always flocked to Lu Jin, including men. Why couldn't she just be more like her friend?

What harm would it be to crash *one* party in her life? Like Elliott said—it would be a great chance for her to meet her new neighbors. Maybe even a chance for her to let her hair down.

She shook her head and chastised herself for even thinking about chucking her responsibility to go somewhere she hadn't been invited.

She stood and laughed at what now seemed a ridiculous idea and returned to the bedroom to finish unpacking her things. No sooner had she returned to her room, did she hear a slight knocking behind her. She jumped and pivoted to the bedroom door.

"Lu Jin." She breathed a sigh of relief. "You scared the heck out of me. What are you doing back?"

"You didn't think I would really abandon you, did you?"

Destiny furrowed her brows and nodded.

Lu Jin covered her heart with her hand. "I'm hurt."

"I'm being honest," Destiny retorted with first a stern face, but then allowed a lopsided grin to slide into place. "But I'm glad you came back."

Lu Jin moved over to her with her arms spread wide, and then embraced Destiny. "Now, I couldn't let my best friend down," she said with an added squeeze of affection. When Lu Jin withdrew, she held up a slender finger. "However, I do think we need to order that pizza before my stomach eats a hole clear to my back."

Destiny laughed. "You got it."

Chapter 3

The next morning, Miles jerked up in bed at the sound of the phone ringing somewhere in the vicinity of his head. He fumbled with the pillows and bumped into a warm body lying next to him. He wondered briefly at the woman's identity before the phone rang again.

This time the noise caused his temples to pound. For a fleeting moment he wanted to throw it and the now-snoring mystery woman out of the room so he could return to his dream of a harem of gorgeous women.

Finally, his hand hit something hard beneath the sheets and managed to pluck the phone from the numerous folds of material and answer it before the caller was sent to his answering machine.

"Hello." He winced at the sound of his brassy voice. He coughed, trying to clear his throat, but only succeeded in igniting a small fire that burned through his larynx.

"Hello, yourself." The sound of his mother's sharp and agitated voice had no trouble penetrating the thick haze around his brain. "Is it too much trouble for a mother to ask her son to help with a few minor chores around the house? I mean, if it is, just let me know and I won't trouble you any more than I have to."

Miles moaned and fell back against the pillows.

His mother's voice raised an octave. "Hello. Are you still there?"

"Yes. I'm still here." He sighed heavily, then managed to pry his eyes open to look over at the clock. "Mom, it's only ten. I have plenty of time to get over there and check out that leak."

"Please. You have to get up, shower, get rid of the woman that is undoubtedly lying beside you and eat breakfast before you get anywhere near your car to come over here."

Regardless of his headache, Miles couldn't help but emit a low rumble of laughter. "Calm down, Mom. I'm getting up right now."

On cue, his mother sighed deeply into the phone, and then started her weekly spiel. "I don't understand how come you can't just find yourself a nice girl to settle down with and stop all this bed-hopping you do. Don't you know how dangerous it is nowadays to be doing that sort of thing?"

"Yes, Mom." Miles stood and glanced down at the women in his bed. So, he had ended up with the curvaceous woman in red after all. He smiled, and then turned away from the bed and headed toward the bathroom. His smile disappeared when his attention returned to his mother shouting over the phone. "Yes, Momma. I hear you. And no, I'm not interested in meeting your bridge partner's daughter."

"It's that Wes character, isn't it?" his mother continued on. "I've been telling you since you two were in junior high that that boy is a bad influence. I wish you would just stop hanging around him. His father was no good and you mark my words that the apple doesn't fall too far from the tree."

Miles's smile widened. If anything, he was the bad influence and always had been. However, he wasn't about to tell his mother that. "Wes is cool. You'd like him if you got a chance to know him better."

"I don't want to know him better. In fact, while I'm thinking about it, I'm not too crazy about most of your friends."

Miles continued to smile against the phone while he wrenched open the medicine cabinet and retrieved the bottle of aspirin.

"Really, Miles. How come you can't find better friends?"

"I know this may come as a surprise to you, but I happen to like my friends."

"Humph."

Miles laughed. "Let's just agree to disagree on the matter."

"Fine. Have you thought any more of taking your cousin Fred's case?"

Here we go. "Why don't we talk more about that when I get there," he stalled.

"There's nothing to talk about. He's family. Family takes care of family."

"We're not the mafia. Besides, we barely know that side of the family. For all we know, he may be the sort of man to harass an employee."

"Oh, I don't believe that."

Miles turned on the shower. "How can you be so sure? When was the last time you talked to Aunt Elise, let alone visited her and her son?" Miles stopped. "Come to think of it, I thought you and Aunt Elise had a falling out a few years ago?"

"Water under the bridge."

Miles shook his head. "We'll talk about this when I get there."

"Fine. Try to make it here at a reasonable hour. The girls are coming over for a game of bridge."

"Deal." Miles disconnected the call. His mother was something else and he loved every bit of her. She was either eccentric or nutty as a fruitcake—it all depended on one's perspective. He believed she kept him grounded—to a certain extent.

He remembered the loving stories his father told him of how and when he'd fallen in love with the wealthy Violet Somers. His father said he was the envy of all his friends. He was also certain his love for Violet would break any silly notions of a family curse.

Miles stepped into the shower and hung his head low beneath the steady stream of hot water. A familiar ache rose within him and pounded in time with his heartbeat. He missed his father, more so now than ever. Everyone kept saying time healed all wounds—but time was the one thing he didn't have a lot of.

Destiny rose early, despite the fact she'd only gotten three hours of sleep. By eight, she'd already eaten her breakfast, depleted her third cup of coffee and finished reading the morning paper. Now, she sat pecking away on her laptop, working on a legal brief that, according to her personal schedule, needed to be done by Monday.

A soft knock on the door drew her attention. She glanced at her watch and was excited to see that it was ten.

She sprinted from the table to answer the door, but was taken aback by an angry woman.

"Where is he?" the woman demanded and pushed her way into the apartment.

"Wait a minute. What in hell do you think you're doing?" Destiny demanded in equal measure.

The woman settled her hands on her hips while her gaze raked over Destiny. "So who are you, his latest conquest?"

"What?" Destiny shook her head. "You know, I don't even care what you're talking about. You have exactly ten seconds to get out of my apartment before I call the cops."

"I'm not leaving here until I talk with Miles."

Destiny held fast to her temper. "You have the wrong apartment. Mr. Stafford lives across the hall."

The woman's color drained as her mouth dropped open and formed a perfect circle.

Destiny pulled the door open farther. "This is the part where you leave."

"I'm so embarrassed."

"With good reason." Destiny gestured toward the door. "Have a good day."

The uninvited guest moved timidly toward the door. She stopped when she reached Destiny and looked as though she wanted to attempt another apology. She walked to the door and nearly collided with someone on the other side.

"Oh, hello."

Destiny recognized her mother's voice outside of the door.

"Hello," the stranger greeted in kind, and then excused herself without any further ado.

Destiny poked her head around the door and smiled at her mother, Adele. "It's about time you got here." She looked around. "Where is Jasmine?" She referred to her mother's feline.

Adele jutted a finger at the woman who had just left the apartment and was now banging on the door across the hall. "A friend of yours?"

"Not hardly. Come on in."

Adele crossed the threshold into the apartment just as the door across the hall jerked open.

"Gina."

Adele and Destiny turned toward the startled male voice in the hallway.

Gina pushed her way into Miles's apartment, yelling at the top of her lungs.

Miles poked his head out into the hallway and his gaze swept toward Destiny and her mother. He gave them an embarrassed smile. "Good morning, ladies."

"I knew it!" Gina's voice reached a new octave.

Miles rolled his eyes, and then ducked back into his apartment just as the sound of two women's voices filled the hallway.

Adele turned toward her daughter.

Destiny could only shake her head. "Please don't ask." She shut the door behind her mother, but they were still able to hear the commotion across the hall. "How ghetto is that?"

"You told me not to ask."

Destiny shook her head determined to put all thoughts of her philandering neighbor aside, but failed. "That man is something else."

"He is a handsome devil. I'll give him that much."

"And milking it for all it's worth. I've been here less than twenty-four hours and I already don't like him."

Adele looked at her daughter with a spark of curiosity. "Is that so?"

Destiny frowned. "What?"

"Nothing." Her mother shrugged, and then moved past Destiny to head for the kitchen. "I sure hope you have a pot of coffee on. I'm ready for a caffeine fix."

"A caffeine fix? You've been watching too much TV."

"Agreed. Which is why I intend to go on a seven-day vacation and I want you to go with me."

"Come again?" Destiny followed her mother into the kitchen. "You know I can't do that. I just started a new job and have been handed my first case. I can't just pick up and leave right now."

"How do you know unless you ask?"

Destiny plopped her hands on her hips. "You've got to be kidding me, right?"

Adele threw her hands up as if frustrated by some unknown burden, but she remained mute to whatever was troubling her.

"What's wrong, Mom?"

"Nothing's wrong. Can't a mother want to spend time with her daughter if she wants? I hardly see you anymore. And since your father passed way, the house…"

Destiny watched the shift of emotion on her mother's face. "What about the house?"

Adele's transformation was nearly complete. Twice before Destiny had seen this fragile, almost vulnerable side of her mother. The first time was when she'd learned of Adam's death, and then again as she stood beside her husband's casket.

"The house is so empty…and haunted."

Startled, Destiny blinked; sure she hadn't heard her correctly. "What do you mean haunted?"

Adele gave an embarrassed laugh and shook her head. "I don't mean I see ghosts roaming around the house or anything like that. I just mean…" She shook her head and took a deep breath. "I have memories in every corner of that house. Some good ones and some bad." She lowered her gaze, suddenly fascinated by her hands.

Destiny's heart went out to her.

"It's funny," Adele went on to say. "I always thought I'd cherish those memories. Now, I dread whenever I turn a corner—afraid one day I'll see your father standing there."

"Or Adam?" Destiny asked.

Adele's head snapped up. Her gaze locked with her daughter's. Before she could speak, tears shimmered and trickled over her lashes.

"Oh, Momma." Destiny embraced her mother as if she was a fragile child. "Sometimes I feel as if I'm haunted by them, as well," Destiny confessed. "Why don't you put the house up for sale? There's no need to keep putting yourself through this."

Adele pulled out of her daughter's arms and shook her head. "I considered it, but for the same reasons I dread the memories, I love the house. Your father and I have always loved it there. If I were to sell it now, I'd feel like I was betraying his memory."

"But you have to do something."

"I am," Adele said, wiping at her tears. "I'm taking a vacation and I would like for you to come with me."

Destiny pulled away. "I can't do that. I mean I wish I could, but I simply can't."

Adele drew in a deep breath and nodded in understanding. "Still off to conquer the world?"

"Just determined to make a difference."

"Are you sure that's all?"

Their leveled gazes locked.

Destiny knew her mother didn't understand her motivation to redeem the Brockman name so she did the only thing she could. She lied. "I'm sure."

Chapter 4

Violet Stafford couldn't wait to introduce her new friend, Adele Brockman, as her new bridge partner to the rest of the girls. She was sure they'd love the intriguing widow as much as she.

Violet had met Adele last month at a charity auction and they'd immediately hit it off. After comparing stories, they'd discovered they knew some of the same people and had at one time or another traveled in the same circles. It was a wonder they hadn't met until now.

What fascinated Violet were Adele's stories about her daughter. She sounded positively delightful; smart, pretty and, most of all, *single*. If only Violet could somehow manage to get Miles's mind off family curses and whatnot, and concentrate on settling down and giving Violet what she longed for—grandchildren.

The doorbell rang and jarred Violet out of her thoughts.

She set down the glass pitcher of iced tea and rushed to answer the door.

"Adele," Violet exclaimed with outstretched arms and a heartfelt smile. "I'm so glad you were able to make it."

Adele entered the house and accepted Violet's embrace. "Your directions were great. I had no trouble finding the place." She pulled out of her friend's arms and took in her surroundings while Violet closed the door. "What a lovely home you have."

"Why, thank you. This place was a labor of love for me and my husband—along with our son, of course." Violet's smile faltered when she witnessed a strange shadow cast over her friend's eyes. "What is it? Did I say something wrong?"

Adele waved her off. "Oh, no. Don't be silly. Are the other girls here yet?"

"No. You're the first to arrive. May I take your jacket?"

"Sure." Adele slid out of the tailor-made jacket and handed it over. "Now I want you to be patient with me. I haven't played bridge in quite some time now. So I'm warning you, I may be a little rusty."

"No problem. I'll make sure I tell the girls to take it easy on us."

They laughed.

"Come on, I'll give you the grand tour," Violet said.

"Lead the way."

The tour of the house only took a few minutes and Adele adored everything she saw. She even said she and Violet shared the same taste when it came to decorating.

"So, did you finally mention to your daughter the trip we talked about?" Violet asked when they returned to the living room.

"Yes. In fact, I saw her this morning. I even tried to get her to travel with me."

"She didn't want to go?" Violet asked, amazed.

"It's not so much that she doesn't want to go, but that she can't right now."

"Oh, I'm so sorry. I thought it was a great chance for you to get away."

"I didn't say *I* wasn't going."

Violet brightened. "Well, that's great news."

"I want you to come with me," Adele announced with an uplifted chin.

"What?"

"Why not? You told me your son was busy with his career, and that you had a lot of time on your hands. So why can't we both go off to Belize?"

Violet blinked, and then thought about it. There really wasn't a reason why she couldn't go. In fact, when was the last time she went on a vacation? "You know, you just might be on to something." She glanced at her watch and wondered what was keeping Miles. She wanted to introduce him to Adele. If she liked him, which Violet held no doubts that she would, then Violet would suggest, quite innocently, of course, that their children meet.

Violet hid a slight smile. It really was a good plan now that she thought about it. She glanced at her watch again. Now, if she could just get her slothful son to show up.

After a morning of dealing with his ex-flame's shenanigans, Miles was finally free to check out the leak at his mother's house. The life of a player wasn't as easy as some rap stars made it out to be—but it was damn close.

He stepped outside of his condo and heard the door from across the hall open. He turned in its direction with a ready smile and wasn't the least bit discouraged when he was met with a stern look of disapproval from his new neighbor, Destiny.

"Good afternoon," he greeted.

Destiny sighed, and then belatedly returned his greeting with a great show of disinterest.

Miles resisted the urge to laugh, to do so would probably further irritate the woman. His gaze swept over her attire, a simple white blouse and black slacks. His brows furrowed in curiosity. She'd brushed what he knew to be her long mane into a straight, tight bun that sat neatly pinned at the nape of her neck.

There was something about the way she carried herself that said "hands off" to the casual observer. It was that same quality that intrigued him.

"I want to apologize for what happened this morning," he said. "Gina told me she got our condo's mixed up."

Destiny finished locking her door and turned with a tight smile. "Perhaps I should post a sign on my door directing your harem to the right address."

This time Miles did laugh. "A harem? Hardly."

Destiny shrugged and strode past him in the direction of the elevator bay.

Miles caught a whiff of Channel No. 5 as she passed. *A classic.* He smiled as he followed her. "You know. I'm starting to think we got off on the wrong foot," he suggested as she continued to walk away.

She pushed the down button for the elevator. "Oh, I don't know. I suppose our meeting was pleasant enough," she replied without making eye contact.

"Then how come I get the distinct impression you don't like me?"

His direct question threw her, but she smiled in kind, and then treaded lightly. "I never said that I didn't like you."

"So you *do* like me?" He moved closer and she stepped back.

"I didn't say that, either," she answered, cautiously.

"Then what *are* you saying?" He made sure he kept his gaze leveled and his expression serious.

The elevator arrived and she looked relieved at the sound of the bell. However, the emotion faded when he stepped into the elevator behind her.

"Mr. Stafford," she said in an impressive, diplomatic voice. "I don't know you, so I'm hardly in any position to tell whether I like you."

He laughed. "That's B.S. and you know it." He punched a button on the panel and the elevator jerked to a stop.

"Excuse me?" Her eyes widened in alarm.

He held up his hands. "I don't think either of us should get off this elevator until we settle this matter." He smiled seductively at her. He was at the top of his game and felt he'd win an invitation to her apartment for a cozy dinner and perhaps more by the time they reached the lobby.

"Have you lost your mind?" She turned to the panel on her side of the elevator and pushed for the lobby. The elevator descended again.

Miles pushed another button and once again they stopped. He smiled at her spark of irritation. She was quite beautiful when she was angry. Fleetingly, he wondered if she was a hellcat between the sheets. "So, were you and your girlfriend pulling my leg yesterday or are you two really an item?"

"My relationship with Lu Jin is none of your business," she snapped.

He moved toward her. "I think you two were pulling my leg."

"So what if we were?"

"I knew it." He inched closer.

Her gaze narrowed as her hands went to her purse.

He faltered. "Now wait a minute." He held up his hands again, suddenly sorry for what seemed moments ago a humorous game.

A small canister slid into the palm of her hand. Relieved it wasn't a gun, Miles stepped toward her, seeking a different avenue to placate her when her arm extended toward him and, before he could say anything else, she sprayed.

Pain, unlike anything he'd ever felt before, ripped through his head. He fell to the floor with a cry of alarm that turned into a wail. His eyes were on fire. Had she blinded him for life? He rubbed fiercely at his eyes, but the more he rubbed the worse it got.

The elevator descended while he writhed on the floor. He wanted to yell at her—worse, he wanted to wring her neck; but all he could manage to do was wail endlessly.

A bell rang and the elevator doors slid open.

"Have a nice day, Mr. Stafford," Destiny said above his cries and stepped out of the elevator.

"Heavens. I just don't know what's keeping that son of mine," Violet said abruptly, interrupting the idle chatter among her bridge group.

"Oh, I didn't know you were expecting Miles today," Leona, Violet's oldest friend, said. "I know it's been a while since I've seen him. How is he liking everything at Mortensen and Foster?"

"Fine, fine. He claims they're keeping him busy." Violet smiled despite her growing frustration.

"Mortensen and Foster?" Adele asked. "Is your son a lawyer?"

Violet perked up. She may have to sell Adele on Miles without her having the opportunity to introduce him to her. "Oh, yes. He's a brilliant attorney. I'm quite proud of him."

Another shadow fell over Adele's features, but vanished just as fast.

"It's amazing how much we have in common," was her

reply, but there was something that wasn't being said. Violet was sure of it.

"Didn't you say your daughter was a lawyer?" Kathleen, another old friend of Violet's, asked Adele, joining in on the conversation.

Adele perked up. "Yes, I did. Actually, she's starting a new job with Phillips, Anderson and Brown on Monday."

The small group of women exchanged impressed looks.

"Is she married?" Leona asked.

Violet shifted. Leona's affluent son had just filed for his fourth divorce and Violet could already see the wheels churning in her friend's head.

"No." Adele's smile hinted at something. "Not yet anyway."

Violet's spirits plummeted. "What do you mean?"

"Well, an old friend of mine has a son, Jefferson Altman, who has expressed interest in meeting Destiny. So we've arranged a way for the two to meet tomorrow."

"Oh?" Violet gave her a half smile, but felt like kicking herself. Someone had already beaten her to the punch.

"I think it's quite exciting. I never played Cupid before. I just hope they like each other." Adele laughed. "Of course I also hope Destiny is compliant. She can be a bit stubborn when she wants. She inherited that trait from her father."

The girls laughed, everyone except for Violet. The small voice in her head told her that she may be down, but she was definitely not out. All she needed to do was pray that this Jefferson Altman and Destiny wouldn't hit it off. *Be patient, Violet—just be patient.*

Chapter 5

It should be against the law to subject people to visits to the emergency room, Miles thought bitterly. In less than two minutes, the staff deemed his case a nonemergency, so he and Wes waited—and waited—for a doctor.

"Cheer up." Wes chuckled and slapped Miles hard across the back. "At least we know now you're not going to be blind for life."

Miles's jaw clenched. Three hours ago he'd been convinced otherwise. He had no real memory of how Wes was called to his aid, but at the time, he'd been grateful.

"So when are you going to fess up and tell me what happened between you and your next-door neighbor?"

"I would think that was obvious."

"How about the events leading up to her whipping your butt?"

"Yeah, right," Miles snapped.

Wes swiveled in his chair and faced Miles. "Any time a woman leaves a man withering on the floor and crying for his momma—he got his ass kicked." Wes laughed. "I swear I wouldn't have believed it if I hadn't seen you with my own eyes. I can't wait to meet this chick."

"Go to hell, Wes."

Wes snapped his fingers. "I bet she's the butch in the relationship."

"What?" Miles shook his head at the direction the conversation had turned.

"A butch," Wes said again. "You never heard of that term?"

"Enlighten me," Miles said, wanting to hear what Wes would say.

"Well, don't quote me on this, but I heard in lesbian relationships there's always a masculine and feminine partner. The masculine is referred to as the butch."

"Where do you get this stuff?"

"Hey." Wes shrugged. "I hear things."

Miles rolled his eyes. "What's so bad is that you repeat them."

"Whatever. I wasn't the one who just got beaten down by a woman. Do you know what a thing like this could do to a man's reputation?"

Miles turned toward him. "You know there is one good thing about being at the hospital."

"What's that?"

"When I beat the hell out of you, you won't have far to go for medical care."

Wes held his hands up in surrender. "Point taken."

Two hours later, with nothing more than a bruised ego, Miles and Wes returned to their high-rise building. When the elevator's door slid open on the fourteenth floor, Miles immediately noticed the tall, slender beauty knocking on Ms. Brockman's door.

Lu Jin turned in his direction.

Wes tilted his shades down. "Have mercy, have mercy," he mumbled under his breath.

They stepped out of the elevator and Lu Jin moved toward them. "My goodness, what happened to you? You look like you've been run over by a Mack truck."

Miles approached his apartment door. "You mean your little girlfriend didn't tell you what happened?"

Wes cleared his throat.

Miles glanced over his shoulder and picked up on the hint. "Wes, Lu Jin. Lu Jin, Wes."

Wes turned with a ready smile. "How do you do?"

Lu Jin smiled, but continued with her interrogation. "Are you saying that Destiny had something to do with this?"

"She attacked him with a can of pepper spray," Wes explained for his pal.

Miles glared at him.

"What?" Wes asked stupefied. "She's going to find out sooner or later."

Miles pushed open his door and entered.

Wes looked to Lu Jin. "I think your girlfriend bruised his ego."

Ignoring Wes, Lu Jin followed Miles to the threshold of his apartment. "So what did you do to her?"

"Me?" Miles thundered, incredulous. "I didn't do anything. The girl has a screw loose or something."

"Come on. I've been best friends with Destiny since college and she doesn't go around spraying innocent people with pepper spray without a damn good reason."

"You mean your girlfriend, right?" Wes continued to weave his way into the conversation.

Annoyed, Lu Jin exhaled. Slowly, she turned toward Wes, with her hands cradling her hips. "I mean just what I said, Wes."

Miles suspected that Lu Jin wanted to call Wes something other than his Christian name.

Wes didn't seem to notice her agitation as he looked back over at Miles. "Clears things up for me. What about you?"

"Crystal. Now if you two don't mind. I would like to get some rest."

"You're not going to tell me what you did to Destiny?"

Miles reined in his temper. "I didn't do anything to your friend. She survived our little meeting unscathed."

"Then why isn't she home?"

It was getting harder for Miles to hide his irritation. "Do I look like her babysitter?"

Lu Jin stepped back as he approached her.

"But when you do see your best friend again, tell her she's lucky I don't drag her skinny butt into court for that stunt she pulled today."

Lu Jin backed silently out into the hallway.

Miles didn't like the uncertainty he read in her eyes. It was the second time today a woman had looked at him with a spark of fear and it unnerved him. At the same time, he didn't have a firm grasp on his anger so he abandoned any hoped to placate her.

"Goodbye," he said, and then closed the door.

"Well, I guess you just told her," Wes said, coming out of Miles's kitchen toting a beer.

"You can leave, too," Miles informed him. It wasn't necessary to sugarcoat anything with Wes. They'd been friends too long for that.

"So this is how you treat a brother who came to your rescue?" Wes smiled, but walked toward the door. "A man should never burn his bridges."

"Yeah, yeah. Whatever."

"All right. I'll holler at ya later." Wes opened the door.

"Later," Miles said, and headed back to the bathroom, where he made a cool compress, and then fell against his bed with the towel draped over his eyes. It had been quite embarrassing to have Wes rush him to the emergency room and have his eyes washed out with saline water.

Destiny's image resurfaced and Miles groaned with disgust. "That woman has to be the devil incarnate," he mumbled.

The phone rang and he considered not answering, but he had a good idea who was calling him. He picked up the receiver. "Hello, Momma."

"What on earth are you still doing home?' she demanded.

"Because some crazy woman emptied a can of pepper spray into my eyes."

"What?"

At least Miles had won a note of sympathy from her.

"What did you do to the poor woman?"

"Me? Why do you suspect that I was the one at fault?"

"Because I know you better than anyone."

"And as my mother you believe that I would do something to a woman that justifies being accosted with a can of pepper spray?"

"Miles, stop being dramatic and tell me what happened."

"I'll tell you what happened. For the first time in my life I met a woman that I absolutely can't stand and wish to hell that I never have to see again."

Chapter 6

Destiny's first day on the job was a whirl of activity. After the usual introductions to the members of Phillips, Anderson and Brown, she was shown to a small office with a dismal view of another looming high-rise. The office came equipped with a beautiful mahogany desk and an exquisite leather chair that was as comfortable as it was stunning.

She could tell upon her first meeting with her personal secretary, Jeanne, a perky-faced blonde, they were going to be a great team. When all the niceties were over, Destiny promptly dove into her work and the day flew by.

Her goal was to make partner at the prestigious firm within seven years. In the next decade she'd pursue politics. A smile fluttered to her lips. It had been Adam's exact plan. She'd loved his ideas on tax and education reform and had now adopted them as her own.

A quick rap on the door jolted her from her pleasant memories. "Come in."

The door pushed open and Jeanne poked her head in and, despite the late hour, gave her a radiant smile that reached her sparkling blue eyes. "A Ms. Stella Fernandez is here to see you."

Destiny looked at her watch and frowned. "It's five o'clock. She's over an hour late."

"She says she got stuck in traffic."

This would make Destiny late for dinner with her friends, but she supposed there was no time like the present to get used to long hours. She sighed. "Send her in," she said, retrieving the folder labeled FERNANDEZ from her in-box. She made a quick scan of its contents before her office door reopened and a beautiful, statuesque, Spanish woman entered.

Destiny stood and welcomed the woman with a firm handshake and a warm smile. "Good afternoon, Ms. Fernandez. I'm Destiny Brockman. You did receive our letter informing you that James Holden has left the firm and that I will be the new attorney handling your case?"

"Sí."

"Well, please excuse the mess. I'm still in the middle of moving in. Won't you have a seat?"

"Gracias," Stella said, with a timid smile, and then took a seat in one of the vacant chairs across from Destiny.

Destiny got straight to the point as she settled back in her chair. "I see here you want to sue your employer for sexual harassment. Is that correct?"

Stella nodded.

Destiny gave her an encouraging smile. "And…" She frowned as she shuffled through the papers. "Who was your employer?"

"I was employed at Nexicon," Stella answered in a thick accent. "I was the president's, Mr. Fredrick Boylan's, personal secretary."

Destiny's eyes brightened with recognition. "Your case is against Mr. Boylan?"

Her client nodded and withdrew a tissue from her purse to blot her eyes. "I had been to three different firms before Mr. Holden agreed to take my case."

"Three?" Destiny's brows furrowed. "What were the reasons the other firms gave for not taking your case?"

Stella's laugh was tainted with odium. "Come on, Señorita Brockman. Fredrick Boylan is a very powerful man and can afford the best attorneys. From what I understand, a Señor Stafford from Mortensen and Foster is representing him."

"Mr. Stafford?" Destiny frowned. "That wouldn't happen to be Miles Stafford, would it?"

Stella tossed up her hands. "See? You've heard of him, too."

Destiny's stomach fell somewhere below her knees. That man was everywhere. "Ms. Fernandez, you came to the right place. I would be delighted to take this case. I'm afraid of neither Mr. Boylan nor Mr. Stafford.'

Stella's face glowed with appreciation. *"Gracias,* Señorita Brockman. *Gracias."*

"No. Thank you." Destiny's smile widened. "I'm actually looking forward to kicking Mr. Stafford's butt in court."

Miles stared at his cousin from across his desk. "So you admit you propositioned Ms. Fernandez?"

Fredrick shrugged as if annoyed for having to answer Miles's questions. "She's a good-looking woman."

"You are aware there are laws prohibiting this type of behavior?" Miles grappled to make some sense of his cousin's logic or maybe he was just having a hard time with the man's indifference. He never understood this kind of preying on women and it unnerved him to be related to this man.

For a moment, his thoughts carried him back to the incident with his new next-door neighbor. Was this the kind of man she thought him to be?

"Freddie, I don't know. I'm not real comfortable about this, especially since you're admitting guilt. Maybe you should just consider settling out of court."

Fredrick laughed. "Come on. This is a simple case of her word against mine. Besides, we both know the difference between sexual harassment and a pick-up line is whether the woman finds you attractive."

"And in this case Ms. Fernandez did not."

"She was playing hard to get, trust me on that. The only reason she's suing is because I moved on."

"And you fired her."

"So? She was a lousy secretary."

Miles felt the beginnings of a headache.

Fredrick smiled, clueless of the stress he caused his cousin. "So, how is Aunt Violet doing? I haven't seen her in a while."

Miles managed a half smile. "She's doing good." *That is until I get my hands on her for getting me into this.*

Fredrick stood and adjusted his suit. It was amazing how a three-thousand-dollar Armani suit did nothing to hide his true nature.

"Anyway, I have it on good authority that Ms. Fernandez has had a bit of trouble finding someone to take her case. Last I heard she had an appointment with the latest rookie over at Phillips, Anderson and Brown."

Miles's stomach turned.

"Come on, cousin. This is easy money for you. Besides, you do know the family decree don't you?"

"Family takes care of family," Miles mumbled under his breath. His headache was now sailing toward becoming a massive migraine. He looked at his cousin and then slowly exhaled. "I'll see what I can do."

Fredrick's smile resembled a smirk. "Great. I trust you'll keep me posted?"

Miles stood from his desk and walked Fredrick to his door. "I want you to know that I'm not one hundred percent sold on this case so I'm not going to make any promises."

"Honesty." Fredrick sounded amused. "I like that."

Since Destiny's prayers of avoiding Miles for the rest of her life would go unheeded, she supposed the opportunity to whip the pompous attorney in court was a great consolation.

Now, back at her apartment, Destiny relayed her day and her version of what happened in the elevator to Lu Jin. "I don't know," Destiny said. "Maybe I should move out of this place."

Lu Jin plopped on the sofa beside Destiny still laughing after listening to her tale. "Now don't be ridiculous. Don't let the creep chase you out."

Destiny lifted her wineglass and looked over at her. "Yeah. I know you're right."

"Actually, it sounds like you handled yourself real well in the elevator. I have no doubts that you can handle him in court, too."

"Thanks for the vote of confidence, but I'd just as well not see the man again. I don't like him."

"So I gathered," Lu Jin said, draping her arm around her friend's shoulders. "But I really do think you're making way too much out of this."

Destiny didn't think so, but she refrained from saying as much and took another sip of wine. "I'm starving. Where are the guys? They should have been here by now."

Elliott and Zack had promised to treat them to Chinese since they'd bailed on Destiny the night of the party and had never returned on the agreed upon hour.

Lu Jin glanced at her watch. "I don't know, but I'll give Zack a ring on his cell phone."

Destiny nearly choked. "He bought a cell phone?"

"Yeah, can you believe it? Poor schmuck is finally getting with the nineties."

There was a knock at the door.

"Finally." Destiny jumped up from her seat and went to answer the door. "It's about time you…"

"Good evening," Miles greeted.

Destiny froze as she took in her neighbor's immaculate presence. If she thought him handsome before, it was nothing compared to what he looked like in a suit.

"Destiny, who is it?" Lu Jin asked, jerking Destiny out of her stupor.

"I-it's, uh." She blinked, and then noticed the lopsided grin sloped across Miles's face. "It's nobody."

His smile disappeared.

She pushed him back and stepped out into the hall. "What are you doing here?" she asked in an angry whisper.

He held up a manila folder. "Imagine my surprise when I received this today." He lowered the folder, and then crossed his arms. "I didn't know you were an attorney. Though after experiencing your sense of justice firsthand, I shouldn't be surprised."

Destiny frowned. "Did you just insult me?"

Miles smiled again. "Ms. Brockman, I didn't come here to fight. I merely thought we could discuss this case over dinner. And maybe I can get you to accept my apology for my behavior yesterday in the elevator. Who knows, perhaps we could even resolve the Boylan case quickly and, hopefully this time, painlessly."

Destiny crossed her arms and evaluated her opposition. "Mr. Stafford, I accept your apology, but I'm going to be frank with you. I don't like you and I don't appreciate you dropping by my home after hours to discuss work."

Destiny noticed a twitch along Miles's jawline.

"Do you ever get tired of playing Ms. Hardass?" he asked. His eyes darkened as they narrowed on her.

"Who's playing?"

Miles stepped back as if he didn't trust himself around her. "All right. We'll play this your way. I'll just call my client and tell him that you refused to hear our offer."

"What offer?"

"Oh? You're interested now?"

Destiny clenched her jaw and reined in her irritation. "I'm not in the position to accept or turn down anything, Mr. Stafford. You know that. If you want to talk business then come by my office tomorrow. I'd appreciate it if you called first. You think you and your cousin can do that?"

Miles paused. "How did you know that we're related?"

A wicked sense of pleasure filled Destiny at seeing his surprise. "One thing to remember about me, Mr. Stafford—I always do my homework. See you in court." She turned and reentered her apartment with a wide smile of satisfaction.

Miles entered his condo wanting to throw something. That damn woman had a way of getting under his skin. Until he'd met Destiny, he was convinced he had a certain way with women. Once, he would have considered her behavior a challenge. Now, he considered it annoying as hell.

His phone rang. He glanced at the caller ID and mumbled under his breath before he snatched it up. "Hey, Freddie."

"So did you talk to her?"

"Yes and no. I'll have my secretary get us on her calendar tomorrow, but I don't have a good feeling about this. I don't think Ms. Brockman is easily intimidated."

Fred sighed wearily into the phone. "You're not going to suggest that I settle again are you?"

The fact that this case was weak at best worried Miles, and his suspicion of Destiny being a tough opponent worried him more. The only thing his cousin had in his favor was his money, and with Destiny Brockman that wouldn't be enough.

"Miles, are you still there?"

"Yeah, I'm still here." He glanced back at his door and hoped there would come a day when he would get another opportunity to go against Ms. Brockman. And if he did, he wouldn't turn and run. "Freddie, I hate to be the bearer of bad news, but either you settle out of court or get yourself a new attorney."

Then a funny thing happened...

Chapter 7

Five years later...

Destiny sat bundled in the middle of her bed with a near-empty quart of ice cream and stared dully at the television, which was all she'd been able to do for the past week. Soon after her thirtieth birthday, she'd come to the conclusion she hated everything about her life.

The job she'd once thought to be a dream had turned out to be a nightmare. The job hadn't changed, she had; and that fact opened a floodgate of emotions with guilt riding the high tide.

The phone rang.

Destiny closed her eyes and wished that everyone would leave her alone. In her heart, she knew they were just concerned, but she wanted time to sort things out.

The answering machine picked up and her mom's worried voice filled the room.

"Destiny, this is your mother calling. I don't know what's

going on or why you haven't been at work all this week, but I've made arrangements to take the first flight back home tomorrow morning—"

Destiny snatched up the phone. "That won't be necessary."

"There you are. Where have you been?" Adele snapped. "I've been worried sick."

"I'm sorry." Destiny drew in a deep breath and pressed the mute button on the remote control. "I didn't mean to worry you. I just…" She shrugged and a thick silence hung over the line.

"I'm coming home," her mother declared.

"No, Mom, no." Destiny exhaled. "There's nothing wrong. I'm just taking some time to reevaluate my priorities."

"Does this have anything to do with the Nissel case?"

It had everything to do with Keith Nissel; a pro bono case where her young client was accused of murder, when all he was guilty of was being in the wrong place at the wrong time. She'd slaved over the case, trying to win a stay of execution from the Supreme Court.

But she had lost.

"No, Mom. This has nothing to do with Keith Nissel."

"I don't believe you."

Destiny responded with a note of desperation. "Mom, please. I need some time to sort things out. That's all. I promise I'll call you if I need you to come home."

Once again silence stretched between them before her mother finally acquiesced. "You promise to call?"

Destiny nodded and fought the next tidal wave of tears. "I promise." She ended the call and fell back across the bed exhausted. Maybe she was coming down with something. If so, then perhaps there was a pill she could pop to soothe her woes.

The Nissel case wasn't the first one she'd lost, but it was the first with such deadly results.

She rolled back to the center of the bed and stared up at the ceiling. Something was definitely wrong. In her career, she'd accomplished everything she'd set out to do. Her boss had recently told her she was on the fast track to making partner. Once upon a time, such praise would've had her floating on cloud nine—but not now. In fact, it had the opposite effect.

Maybe the simple truth was she no longer wanted to be a lawyer. Destiny groaned as she slammed her eyes shut. To even consider such a thing deepened her despair. She'd come from a long line of lawyers. And because of the scandal her brother had caused, it was up to her to redeem the family name.

She allowed the last declaration to ring in her ears and waited for the words to revive conviction in her heart. But nothing happened. Nothing had happened for a while.

The doorbell rang.

Destiny held her breath as if doing so would convince her visitor she wasn't home. She prayed she wouldn't hear a key rattle in the door. If she did, it could only mean that her dear friend, Lu Jin, had taken it upon herself to come check on her.

A key rattled.

Destiny grabbed a pillow and covered her face to muffle a scream of frustration.

"Destiny?" Lu Jin's concerned voice floated throughout the apartment.

Destiny removed the pillow. "Go away."

The front door closed and she heard the soft clicking of high heels as they headed toward her room.

Lu Jin stopped when she reached the bedroom door. She crossed her arms and glanced around. "I wouldn't have believed it if I hadn't seen it with my own eyes."

Destiny sat up and propped her pillow against the headboard. "I want my key back."

"People in hell want iced water."

They gave each other a sour look.

"When was the last time you cleaned this place up?" Lu Jin moved farther into the room, carefully stepping over piles of clothes.

"I forget."

Lu Jin sat on the edge of the bed and jumped when she heard something crumple beneath her. She removed a pack of crackers and sat down again. "All right. Enough games. What's bothering you?"

"Nothing. Since when is it against the law to vegetate in the privacy of one's home?"

"Why are you snapping at me? Because I'm concerned?"

Lu Jin always had a way of dancing around Destiny's anger.

"I'm just taking some time out to reevaluate my life. No big deal." Destiny cringed. She was beginning to sound like a broken record.

"Reevaluate? That sounds like guilt or regret talking. What do you have to feel guilty about?"

"Nothing, Lu Jin. You know my life is *perfect,*" she sneered.

"I don't know about perfect, but from where I stand it don't look too shabby." She shrugged while she thought about it. "In a few years you should make partner. You're engaged to Jefferson Altman—*gorgeous* Jefferson Altman, I may add."

"You marry him, since you think so highly of him."

Lu Jin frowned. "It's been a while since I've seen you like this." She leaned forward and placed a hand over Destiny's forehead, which was promptly slapped away.

"Stop it. I don't have a fever."

"Come on. Talk to me."

Another smart retort crested Destiny's tongue, but she managed to prevent it from tumbling out. Through the brief ensuing silence Destiny could feel her friend's heavy gaze follow her every move. She had no choice but to confess. "I thought I could take his place. I want to fulfill his dreams, but I don't think I can do it anymore."

Lu Jin pulled away. "Who are you talking about?"

Destiny read suspicion in Lu Jin's face and knew her answer wouldn't come as a total surprise. "Adam. Who else?"

Miles returned to his condo after completing a four-mile run. It was just what he needed to relieve his stressful week and begin a fun-filled weekend. He closed the door and made a beeline to the refrigerator where he grabbed a nearly empty bottle of Gatorade and drained it.

He glanced at his watch and assessed it shouldn't take him more than half an hour to shower and change. As he headed toward the bedroom, he pushed the play button on the answering machine.

"Hey, buddy. Wes here. I was just calling to make sure we're still on for the night. Donna has already called me half a million times to make sure I have a date for her cousin. I'm counting on you so hit me on my cell when you get this message."

Miles smiled at the note of desperation in his best friend's voice and knew just where Wes was coming from. They had pulled the same favor for each other more times than either cared to remember. Generally, he had a good time with the women his buddy set him up with, probably because they shared the same taste in women—the no-fuss, no-strings-attached type.

Of course, his mother still plagued him about settling down. Her efforts grew more desperate as the years rolled by, but Miles had no intention of sentencing another child to the Stafford curse.

In the shower, he relished the water's pulsing rhythm and allowed himself to wonder what his date looked like. Exactly thirty minutes later, Miles was ready to go. He gave the place a quick once-over, pleased that the maid service had once again done a splendid job and placed fresh flowers throughout the apartment—women love flowers.

Snatching up his keys, he headed out the door and was surprised when he came face-to-face with his old nemesis, Jefferson Altman.

A wide, even smile cracked Jefferson's usually stoic features as his brown eyes turned coal black in an instant.

Jefferson tilted his head in a light greeting. "Stafford."

"Altman," Miles mimicked, hating how the man had always insisted on calling him by his last name as though they were in the military.

Since their college days they'd managed to stay out of each other's way until Altman started dating Miles's next-door neighbor. Truth be told, he didn't know which person he pitied more. Then again, maybe Destiny and Jefferson were an ideal couple.

Miles locked his apartment door and headed toward the elevator bay without further comment. When he walked away, his thoughts traveled to his neighbor. For the past five years, they'd managed, and exceptionally well, to avoid each other—except in the mornings. She was usually headed out to work about the same time he was leaving for his morning jog.

The elevator arrived at the same time Jefferson announced himself through Ms. Brockman's door.

Miles frowned and searched his memory for the last time he'd seen Destiny. He couldn't remember seeing her all week. How odd.

He stepped into the elevator, and then watched as Altman entered the apartment. For the first time, Miles noticed the flowers Altman carried.

Miles shrugged. Maybe Destiny had caught a bug or something. Anyway, it was none of his business.

* * *

Lu Jin returned to Destiny's bedroom and declared in an excited whisper. "It's Jefferson."

Destiny buried her face within the pillows again and screamed. Jefferson Altman—*boring* Jefferson Altman was the last person she wanted to see. "Tell him I'm sick."

"What?" Lu Jin removed the pillows. "Destiny, get up. You're acting ridiculous. If you hate your life so much then get up and do something to change it."

Destiny stared at her. In one sentence Lu Jin had the solution to her problems; so simple in its concept, and yet difficult in its application.

"Well?" Lu Jin settled her hands on her hips. "Are you going to get up or am I going to send him back here to this pigsty?"

It wouldn't do any good to call Lu Jin's bluff. Her friend always said what she meant and meant what she said, so Destiny threw back the covers and pulled herself out of bed.

"That's my girl. Now, I'll go tell him you're coming," Lu Jin gushed, and then rushed out of the room.

Despite the overpowering urge to dive back into bed, Destiny shuffled her way to the adjoining bathroom to make herself presentable. However, when she stood in front of the mirror, she didn't feel like prettying herself up and pretending that everything was okay—far from it. She just wanted to be left alone where she could start on another quart of ice cream.

She looked down with a certain detachment at the simple diamond ring glittering on her finger. She had no right to accept a ring from a màn she didn't love. He was, however, a man she cared for—but that wasn't enough anymore.

Destiny went to her living room still dressed in her frumpy pajamas and with her hair pointing in every direction. There was a horrified gasp from Lu Jin and Destiny watched as Jefferson's expression fell.

Maybe this wasn't a good idea. "Hey," she said with a ghost of a smile.

Jefferson and Lu Jin exchanged looks before Lu Jin bailed out.

"Well, I think I'll leave you two lovebirds alone."

Destiny thought to stop her, but knew it was because she wanted emotional support for what she was about to do.

"I'll call you later," Lu Jin said, waving from the door, and then slipped out.

Destiny felt as if she had been cast in a commercial; if a pin dropped, she was certain it would sound like a car crash.

"I brought these for you." He awkwardly extended a bundle of carnations.

She smiled and stepped forward to accept them. "They're lovely."

Jefferson slid his hands into his pockets and rocked on his heels. "Is everything…okay?" he asked.

Destiny drew in a deep breath and danced around his question. "Things could be better." He'd never been a good shoulder to cry on. His involvement with her was nothing more than a power move on his part. She was a sort of intellectual trophy to drag to one social function after another in order to help elevate his career. And he was the same for her.

Jefferson cleared his throat. "Well, I was beginning to worry about you when you hadn't returned any of my calls this week, but it's good to see—" he swallowed and looked uncomfortable "—that you're okay."

Destiny rolled her eyes and turned away. "I'll go put these in some water." This definitely wasn't going to be easy.

Miles wanted to kill Wes and go home—in that order. Miles's date, Lakenya, or something to that effect, seemed nice enough—until she got a few drinks in her. Then she was loud—bullhorn loud and way too touchy-feely.

Wes, on the other hand, was having a grand old time with Donna Klein and was ignoring every signal Miles tossed his way.

"So tell me how a woman hasn't dragged a fine brother like you down the aisle by now?" Lakenya blew a stream of smoke out the side of her mouth.

Miles entertained thoughts of dying from second-hand smoke inhalation. At least it would end the date on a high note. "I don't know. I've just been lucky, I guess."

"You mean lucky for me." She eased closer, giving Miles a good whiff of alcohol and cigarettes.

Miles smiled despite himself.

"So how are you two making out?" Wes finally managed to drag his eyes away from his date long enough to ask.

Miles didn't blame him. Donna was hot and the total opposite of her outlandish cousin. "We're doing just fine." He made sure sarcasm dripped from each word.

Wes pretended not to notice.

"Hey." Lakenya directed Miles's chin toward her. "How about a dance?"

His brain screamed no, but she was already out of her chair and pulling him along with her. There were a few gazes that swung their way from both sexes when Lakenya passed. It was most likely because Lakenya was a size twelve squeezed into a size eight dress.

Once they were on the dance floor, he tried to lose himself in the music, but was instead irritated by the crowded dance floor and hard-driving bass booming from the speakers. With his fortieth birthday looming on the horizon, he was beginning to feel he was getting too old for the club scene.

Lakenya grabbed his attention, or rather his butt, and then flirted with more than mere body language.

"My cousin told me to watch out for you," she said, leaning up to his ear.

"Oh, really?"

"Yeah. But I don't know. As good as you look I may just have to take my chances."

"Is that right?" He laughed, but felt like crying. It was definitely going to be a long night.

Chapter 8

"You're giving back my ring?" Bewildered, Jefferson stared down at the diamond in his hand.

Destiny nodded and wiped at a stray tear. "I'm sorry. I know this must come as a surprise and I'm sorry that I don't have this long, wonderful speech on what went wrong." She was rambling again, she realized. It was a habit she'd picked up from her mother. However, she needed to get this over with while she still had the courage.

Jefferson nodded as if he understood, but his confusion remained evident in his expression.

Her heart squeezed. Jefferson had been nothing but kind and patient. For more than a year he'd waited for her to pin down a wedding date when all along she'd been thinking of ways to do just this—break up with him. In the past few months, they'd even gone as far as to go house hunting.

"Was it something I did?" he asked. When she hesitated

to answer, he went on. "Because I thought we were perfect together. I mean, we want the same things."

Destiny lowered her gaze and asked him an important question. "Jefferson, are you in love with me?"

The lengthy silence forced her to look at him again. His Adam's apple bobbed incessantly as he struggled for the right response.

"We'd agreed that our pairing was based on mutual respect. I mean, we complement one another—our ambitions, our lifestyles," he finally said.

She nodded and even managed to smile. "I know that's what we said, but that's not enough for me anymore. I need—I deserve more than that."

He swallowed and looked as if he still had a hard time processing everything. "When did all of this change—yesterday or last year?"

It was a loaded question and she knew it. "I don't know."

"I see." He closed his hand around the ring and slipped it into his pocket. "Well, I guess I should leave, then."

She should say something else, but she feared it would only make matters worse.

He turned and she followed him demurely to the door. It was possibly the last time she'd see him and a sudden sense of loss engulfed her.

They exchanged awkward smiles. When she closed the door behind him, Destiny slumped against it and ignored the sting of fresh tears. Was this some kind of midlife crisis she was going through? She shook her head. That didn't make any sense, she wasn't in the middle of her life; she was still young and vibrant. "Oh, who am I kidding?"

She pushed away from the door and shuffled back toward the bedroom. Maybe this was early menopause; maybe tomorrow she'd wake up and realize she'd made a terrible mistake.

Her heart skipped a beat and she stopped in her tracks as

a ball of anxiety rolled heavily in the pit of her stomach. Jefferson was right. Their relationship had never been based on love; it had been based on a commonality. They were both career driven and motivated.

"Dear God. What have I done?" Destiny pivoted, rushed back to the door and then jerked it open. "Jefferson!" she shouted down the hall.

He was gone.

She raced to the elevator bay and frantically stabbed the down button. If she hurried she could catch him in the lobby or at least before he left the parking deck.

An elevator arrived and she jumped in.

Seconds later, Lu Jin returned to the fourteenth floor in a different elevator. "I must have left my keys on the bed," she mumbled under her breath. When she reached Destiny's door, she made a quick knock, and then entered. "Hello, it's just me." Silence greeted her. With no sight of either Destiny or Jefferson, Lu Jin hesitated to move toward the bedroom.

She smiled. Apparently, they had patched up their differences. "Hey, Destiny, it's me," she called out. "I think I left my keys in your bedroom." She waited and frowned when she didn't receive a response.

She eased toward the bedroom. "Hey, you two lovebirds. I hate to interrupt, but I need my keys." She knocked on the door, anticipating an awkward moment when Destiny opened it.

When no one came, she pressed her ear against the door, and then frowned when she heard no sound. She pushed it open. "Destiny?"

Nothing.

"I can't believe she actually left and didn't lock up." Lu Jin moved into the room, found her keys on the edge of the bed and waltzed out. "Sometimes I swear that girl isn't playing with a full deck," she mumbled as she dashed out the front door, locking it behind her. "She can thank me later."

Destiny hadn't reached the lobby before she came to her senses, not to mention realizing that she was still in her pajamas and sporting a Scary Spice hairdo. Jefferson was gone, out of her life, and it was for the best. What she needed to do right now was get back in bed and curl up with what was left of her ice cream. After all, tomorrow was another day—right?

She nodded in a silent affirmation, and then pressed the button to return to the fourteenth floor. She drew in a deep breath and instantly felt better about her decision.

She waited for the elevator to complete its descent to the lobby, but what she hadn't anticipated was for the small compartment to jerk to a stop and for everything to go black.

"What on earth?" Destiny's heart skipped a beat. Eyes wide, she tried in vain to make out her surroundings. Only the sound of her own strained breathing filled her ears. Shouldn't a back-up generator at least restore the lights?

On cue, the overhead lights flickered on and a ripple of relief coursed through Destiny. She punched a button on the panel with the picture of the fireman's helmet. When she heard nothing, she pressed it several more times.

"Maybe it's a silent signal," she reasoned. *But what if it's not?* She studied the paneling again and pushed the button with a picture of a telephone.

"Hello. Hello."

"Front desk, Wendell speaking."

Destiny exhaled at the sound of a familiar voice. "Wendell, this is Destiny Brockman from fourteen-twenty-six. I seem to be stuck in the elevator."

"Yes, ma'am. I've called the fire department, but we're in the middle of a blackout."

"You mean the entire building?"

"Yes, ma'am. I'm also looking out of the windows and it appears to be the whole city block."

Destiny slumped to the floor. "Then it's possible that our building isn't the only one with jammed elevators?"

Wendell exhaled. "That's a high probability."

"And I could be in here for a while?"

There was another exhalation over the line. "Yes, ma'am."

She refrained from cursing at the young clerk and instead said, "Just do what you can."

"Yes, ma'am. I'll call them again right now."

Ending the call, Destiny's earlier depression returned. "I knew I should have never gotten out of bed."

Lu Jin moved slowly down the stairwell with her hands splayed out before her. At least the power had gone out before she had actually gotten back on the elevator. That would have been a disaster.

To be safe, she removed her high heels, and then resumed descending the stairs. In the end, fourteen flights felt more like forty, but at least she'd made it safely out of the stairwell. When she made her way to the lobby, she was surprised to find it deserted. "If I didn't know any better I'd swear I was lost somewhere in the twilight zone." Quickly, she put her shoes back on and rushed out of the building only to discover the entire city block was dark. "Eerie," she whispered, and then headed off to the parking deck and toward her car.

Miles, Lakenya, Wes and Donna had moved their little party to Bella Rosa, a small, upscale Italian restaurant on the northern side of town. Problem was, Wes wanted to get a private table for just him and Donna and wanted Miles to do the same with Lakenya.

Through it all, Miles smiled, dreaming of the moment when he would get Wes alone and kill him in cold blood. He knew the opportunity would come sooner or later. Women always went to the bathroom together, and when they did, Wes was all his.

The restaurant was packed, which was to be expected on a Friday night. Their names were placed on a waiting list, and a young waitress promised to seat them within the next hour. To pass the time, they moved over to the bar for drinks.

Miles feared if Lakenya had another drink, she would be downright uncontrollable. It wasn't that she was slurring words or couldn't walk, or anything like that. But at the beginning of the date she'd behaved like a virginal bride and now she acted more like Li'l Kim.

To his surprise, she ordered a white zinfandel instead of the harder Kahúa drinks she'd had for most of the night.

"Are you okay?" She leaned in his direction to ask.

"Yeah, I'm fine. I'm sorry if I seem a bit distracted," he said with a kind smile. There was no reason why he couldn't make sure that she enjoyed their date.

She smiled back. "You know, I really had a nice time. It did me good to get away from the kids for a night."

Miles frowned. "Kids?"

She nodded as she accepted her drink. "Yeah, I have three little angels. Meiko, Marco and Milo."

His brows rose with amusement.

"Yeah, yeah. I know. All my friends have gotten onto me about that. But what can I say? I have a thing for names that start with the letter *M*." She winked at him.

Miles laughed. "You're something else, Lakenya."

"That's what they keep telling me."

Sitting on the elevator floor, Destiny rocked her head back against the steel paneling certain that she would never see the light of day again. She thought to call Wendell again, but she'd done that eight times already. The last time she'd talked to him, she learned that she'd been in there for a little more than three hours. She guessed now it was close to four.

She leaned forward, wrapped her arms around her legs and laid her head down against her kneecaps. What was the big rush in getting out of there anyway? It wasn't as if she had anything to do—just sulk and mope around and she could do that right there. Actually, she was doing a pretty good job of it.

"If you hate your life so much then get up and do something to change it," Destiny quoted her friend, then quickly grew exhausted thinking of ways to do just that. The problem was she'd spent so much time trying to be like her brother that she had long since stopped trying to be herself.

Hell, she didn't even know what made her happy anymore. "I definitely need to see a therapist."

She stared at her distorted reflection in the elevator's stainless steel. She was quite a sight. She may even give poor Wendell quite a fright when he finally got the doors open. She laughed, and was startled when the elevator jerked and then proceeded to descend to the lobby.

"Oh, thank goodness." She pulled herself up from the floor and, as an afterthought, tried to press down her unruly hair.

The elevator stopped and the doors slowly slid open, but instead of seeing Wendell, she was startled when Miles Stafford filled the threshold.

Chapter 9

Miles's onyx gaze slowly traveled up the length of Destiny's body and lingered at her hair. "The psycho-chic look suits you."

He, on the other hand, was handsome as always. Annoyed, she stepped out of the elevator and into the dark lobby. "I wish I could say the same for that perfume you're wearing."

Miles sniffed at his clothes and then shook his head. "Lakenya."

"La-what?" She frowned at him. "Having problems finding women with normal names?"

"What, like Destiny? The last time I checked that was a noun, not a proper noun."

"I could say the same about your name." She wrinkled her nose at him, and then turned her attention back to the lobby. "The lights are still out."

"Yeah, they flickered on for a second and then went back out when the elevator opened. Coincidence? I think not."

"I'm not in the mood to deal with you today," she said, shaking her head and moving toward the stairwell. "Have you seen Wendell?"

"Not him or anybody else for that matter. How long have the lights been out on this side of town?"

"About four hours." She moved faster when she realized he was following close behind her.

"You weren't in the elevator all that time, were you?"

"Afraid so."

When he didn't respond, her hackles rose. She stopped abruptly and turned to face him. Just as she suspected, he was laughing.

"You're such a child." She pivoted and stormed through the door of the stairwell. It was even darker in there. "I wonder what happened to cause the lights to be out this long?"

"You're not going to tell me you're scared of the dark are you?"

"Whatever. You just make sure you stay the hell away from my neck."

Miles laughed. "So now you think I'm a vampire?"

"It would explain why women are only seen once at your place, never to be heard from again."

"You never miss a beat, do you?"

She turned and started tackling the next set of stairs. "I just don't trust you, that's all."

"Don't tell me you're still sore for losing the Corbin Scott case six months ago?"

She rolled her eyes and felt her anger over the case return. "The guy was a scumbag, but I suspect you know that already. Birds of a feather flock together."

"You're on a roll this evening."

"What can I say? You bring out the worst in me."

"You mean there's a good side?" He snickered behind her. "Come on, admit it. You're a sore loser."

"Not until you admit that you're an ass," she retaliated.

He laughed. "I don't see what you're so sore at. The way I see it, the score is even between us."

She turned to face him, but found it difficult to make out more than an outline in the darkness. "You're actually keeping score?"

"You're not?"

Of course she was. "No. I think that's a bit childish."

"Sure you do."

She started up the stairs, mumbling under her breath. "Besides," she said suddenly. "I have two cases and a settlement against you."

"You're actually counting the Boylan case?"

"Damn right." She picked up her pace, but he easily managed to match her stride.

Laughing, he said, "Now look who's being childish."

"Like I said—you bring out the worst in me."

"It's nice to know I have *some* effect on you."

Destiny made a sudden stop when she reached another landing and caused Miles to run into her. She jumped from the heat of his touch and instead of questioning it, her temper exploded. "Watch it," she snapped.

"Well, warn someone when you're going to stop like that. Why did you stop anyway?"

"I lost count of what floor we're on."

"Sixth."

"How do you know? You've been running your mouth since we got in here."

"It's called multitasking. I can also pat my head and chew gum at the same time. You want to see?" He maneuvered around her and proceeded to climb the stairs ahead of her.

"You're such an ass."

"So you keep telling me. Has anyone ever told you that you're not the most cheerful person to be around?"

She exhaled and realized she was taking a lot of frustration out on him. "Sorry. It hasn't exactly been a great evening for me."

This time Miles stopped abruptly and Destiny crashed into him. "What? Did you run into something?" she asked.

He turned. "No, but I think there's something wrong with my hearing. Did you just apologize?"

"Oh, go to hell." She stormed around him and took the lead again.

Miles's rich laughter filled the stairwell while a small smile hugged her lips.

A few minutes later, they arrived on the fourteenth floor.

Reacquainted with her leg muscles, Destiny tried her best not to fall out into the hallway in front of Mr. Fitness; however, she did make a mental note to start exercising more.

And as if God was playing some cruel, practical joke, the lights flickered on.

"I guess if we'd waited, we could've taken the elevator," Miles said.

In response, Destiny rolled her eyes and continued her way toward her condo. At this point, she was willing to do just about anything to get back in bed. She heard a jingle of keys from behind her.

"Well, it's been real, it's been fun—"

"But it hasn't been real fun," Destiny beat him to the punch line. She twisted the doorknob and was surprised to find it locked. "What the hell?"

Miles pushed opened his door and stopped. "What is it?"

The lights went out again.

"I don't believe this."

"Is there a problem?"

With the hallway dark, she turned toward the sound of his voice. "My door is locked."

"Where's your key?"

Puzzled, Destiny shook her head. "It has to be inside, but I didn't lock the door when I left."

"Okay."

She caught the note of disbelief in his voice. "I know that sounds strange, but I didn't lock it. I rushed out here trying to catch up with Jefferson."

"Why? Did you scare him away with your new 'do?"

She slammed her hands into her hips. "Very funny. You're just as good a comedian as you are a lawyer."

"Ooh, Scary Spice has claws."

Despite everything, she smiled. "May I use your phone to call Wendell downstairs? I need for him to let me in." When Miles didn't immediately reply, Destiny had a sneaking suspicion that he was laughing at her.

"Say, please," he said.

"No."

"Well, it was worth a try. Come on in."

Destiny smiled in the darkness as she crossed over to his apartment, but stopped at the door. Thin stripes of moonlight filtered through the small slits of the Venetian blinds and made it easier for Destiny to see around the apartment.

Miles stopped and looked back at her. "Aren't you going to come in?"

"I'm thinking."

Crossing his arms, he stared at her from across the room. "You're the one that wanted to use the phone. It's not like I'm twisting your arm."

"You have a cordless?"

"Are you for real? Besides a cordless won't work in a blackout."

She exhaled. Maybe she was taking this to the extreme. "Fine. I'll come in."

"Well, don't do me any favors." He turned, shaking his head.

Destiny entered and instantly caught the fresh scent of

flowers. She drew in a deep breath and smiled. "It smells good in here," she said, deciding that it was okay to pay him a compliment.

"You sound surprised."

"I don't know too many bachelors whose pad smells like a section of the Botanical gardens."

He laughed and he headed back toward her. "It's hard for you to be nice to me, isn't it?"

"You have no idea."

"La telephone, mademoiselle."

"Ah, you speak French?"

"Oui, et toi?"

"No. In fact, you just exhausted my vocabulary in the matter." She accepted the phone. "Thank you."

"Je t'en prie," he said, and then turned away.

Destiny quickly punched in the number for downstairs and waited. After the tenth ring, she disconnected the call and frowned. "I wonder where that boy is."

"Knowing Wendell, he's probably taken this chance to sneak some time away with Angela."

"Who's Angela?"

"Seventeen-year-old in eleven-eighteen."

"You're kidding me?"

"I can't think of a more romantic setting than a city blackout."

"Now how come that doesn't surprise me?"

Miles laughed.

There was a click and then a small flame of light posed over a candle and then another. Soon the entire living room glowed with the soft light.

"You're a candle aficionado, too?"

"No, just a silly romantic."

That won a laugh out of her.

"Don't worry," Miles continued. "For some reason, the mood has deserted me tonight."

She wrinkled her nose at him and swallowed her retort. "How about we just call it a truce for the night?"

He shrugged and Destiny caught herself admiring his body's outline. It wasn't the first time she'd done so. Usually, she'd sneak a peek at him in the morning and admire his discipline. Rain, snow or just plain hot as hell, Miles ran religiously every morning and on Fridays, he would take an additional run in the evenings before getting ready to paint the town red.

"So," he said, looking awkwardly around. "Can I get you something while you wait? Something to drink, perhaps?"

Battling her own uneasiness, she shrugged. "Sure, um, some water would be nice."

"Water it is." He headed toward the kitchen. "Please, make yourself comfortable."

Instantly, Destiny's gaze fell to a large, black leather sofa and thought of the countless women he'd seduced there. Now while she thought about it, the entire room felt like a lion's lair.

With a smug smile, she chose the adjoining wing chair. If he thought he'd snagged another victim, he had another thing coming.

"Ah, here you go," Miles said, suddenly from behind her.

Destiny jumped slightly.

He laughed. "There's no need to be bouncing around like some scared mouse. I'm not going to attack you."

"Said the spider to the fly." Destiny accepted the offered bottle of water. "Thank you. And I'm not scared of you." She lifted the bottle to her lips.

"It's not that I hadn't considered it," he added, and then laughed when she started to choke.

"Very funny." She wiped in vain at the front of her pajama top.

Still laughing, he shrugged. "Hey, I'm just being honest with you."

"I guess there's a first time for everything," she said smugly.

His laughter faded. "I thought we were calling a truce?"

She mimicked his earlier nonchalance. "You started it."

He disappeared into the kitchen and returned to hand her a paper towel.

"Thank you."

"Ooh, manners. Who would have thought?"

"You're doing it again," she warned.

He rolled his eyes and went to the sofa. "I don't know what I'm going to do with you."

Destiny forgot she was sitting next to the phone and jumped at its unexpected ring.

Miles laughed again. "I'm glad to see that you're not scared."

She fought her urge to throw the damn thing at him.

"Hello," he answered, standing up and maneuvering around the long cord.

Destiny leaned back in her chair and once again took in her surroundings while he headed toward the kitchen for some privacy.

"Hey, Wes. Yeah, yeah. I'm sorry I bailed out on you, but you know you were dead wrong for that stunt you pulled on me tonight."

Destiny frowned with curiosity, but continued to pretend that she wasn't listening.

"Does it sound like I'm laughing?" Miles said into the phone. "You know I'll get you back." He listened, and then said, "No, no. I was the perfect gentleman. I drove her back home, said hello to her three Bebe kids, and came home."

Taking another sip of water, Destiny's curiosity waned into disinterest. She continued to look around and was more than impressed with the décor. An extraordinary assembly of bold paintings graced one side of the living room while on the other were more gentle, spiritual paintings. The furniture was bold and masculine while everything else was soft and feminine.

She shook her head and decided that he must have hired a professional decorator because if he had done this; it would imply there was a side to him that she preferred to believe didn't exist.

"Sorry about that," Miles said, rejoining her in the living room. He reclaimed his seat on the sofa, and then asked, "Now where were we?"

"Nowhere." She extended her hand for the phone. "May I try Wendell again?"

"Sure." He handed it to her.

She quickly dialed the number only to be disappointed when there was still no answer. "I think I'm going to cry," she said, hanging up.

"Oh, come on. I thought I was doing a good job of keeping you company." He leaned back with a confident smile.

Destiny couldn't figure out what it was about him that put her on edge, but she did have enough common sense to realize that her behavior toward him was bordering on rude, so she made another attempt to adjust her attitude. "I guess I can't complain."

"Then I guess you were right, there's a first time for everything."

They laughed.

Miles swept a hand toward her. "Since Halloween is a little ways off, what on earth possessed you to roam the halls looking like that?"

Self-consciously, she reached up to touch her hair. She gave him an embarrassed look. "It's a long story."

"I don't have anything planned." He took another gulp

from his bottle and added, "And it doesn't appear that you're going anywhere any time soon, either."

"Good point." She drew in a deep breath and exhaled. "I was trying to catch someone before they left the building."

"Altman?"

She frowned. "How did you know that?"

"You said so earlier, plus I saw him before I left." He shrugged. "So, what did you do—scare the devil out of him looking like that?"

"You're being an ass again."

"I'm just being me."

He flashed her with another smile and damn if she couldn't help but return the gesture. "To answer your question—no. I didn't scare him." She paused. "At least not too badly."

They shared another laugh, but Miles's curiosity didn't fade.

"Then I take it, you two had an argument?"

All traces of Destiny's joviality vanished as a jolt of remorse returned. "Not exactly."

Her answer hung in the air while she was suddenly barraged with uncertainty again. When her moment of reflection was over, she was startled to find Miles studying her.

"What?"

He shrugged. "Nothing."

"That didn't look like a nothing."

Miles shrugged again, but continued to look like he wanted to say something.

"Come on. What is it?" she goaded.

"Well, it's not like it's any of my business…"

"But?" She rolled her hands as a gesture for him to just spit it out.

"But I was just wondering what on earth you see in Jefferson Altman—*boring* Jefferson Altman."

Destiny fell back against the chair with a boisterous laugh.

Then, she couldn't seem to stop. Tears trickled down her face and soon she heard him join in with her. Suddenly, Destiny could feel something was happening between them. When she wiped at her eyes, she knew what it was—they were becoming friends.

Chapter 10

As the night rolled on, Miles and Destiny laughed and swapped stories as though it was the most natural thing in the world.

For Miles, he never thought the day would come when he'd consider Destiny Brockman a friend, and he was pleased to have been wrong. Throughout the night, he smiled at her funky hairdo and wrinkled pajamas, but her ethereal beauty fascinated him.

A few times she caught him staring and they would go through a small vignette of her asking, "What?" and him responding, "Nothing."

While she talked, he felt there was a wall guarding certain areas of her life and he became equally interested in what she said as well as what she didn't.

To make her feel more at ease, he'd turned on an old battery-operated radio and they listened to the Quiet Storm program on the city's popular R & B station.

Had it been another night with a different woman, one could easily mistake the intimate setting as a romantic interlude equipped with soft music and candlelight.

"A few minutes ago you said your brother was a lawyer. Is he no longer practicing?" He handed her a half-filled glass of wine, and then returned to the sofa. When he sat down and looked up at her, he was moved by her profound look of sadness. "I'm sorry. Did I say something wrong?"

One side of her mouth lifted in a poor attempt at a smile. She cleared her throat and lowered her gaze to the blush-colored wine. "My twin brother passed away quite some time ago."

"I'm sorry to hear that." Miles heard and read so much in her simple statement, but he practiced restraint and didn't voice any of the questions that filled his head.

She sipped at her wine. "You know I've been thinking a lot about him lately," she went on to confess.

"Were you two close?" He felt safe in asking.

She nodded and a genuine smile came into focus. "Actually, he was my mentor, my hero and my best friend. I can't begin to tell you how much I miss him."

He smiled. "I think you just did."

When she laughed, Miles could tell by her expression that she was still reminiscing about another time, but there was something else—something he couldn't quite put his finger on. Then, just as suddenly, she pulled out of her deep reverie and looked at him. "How about you? Do you have any brothers or sisters?"

"No," he said with a tinge of regret. "I would've liked one though—maybe an older brother or a younger sister."

"Really? Why?"

He shrugged. "I don't know. Growing up, I remember a lot of my friends having siblings. Of course, they would all complain about them in some shape or fashion, but I always envied them." He shrugged again. "But I do have Wes. We're sort of like brothers, if you take away the fact that my mother hasn't exactly taken a shine to him."

"Why is that?"

"Wes loves wild parties, wild women and just flat out having a wild time."

"Excuse me, but has your mother actually met you?"

Miles laughed. "Well, she thinks he's the bad influence on me."

"When you're really the bad apple, right?"

"I plead the Fifth."

"Good idea. Are you close with your parents?" she asked, taking another sip of wine.

"It's just me and my mom now." He lowered his gaze to his drink. He tried to conjure up an image of his father from memory and was saddened by how difficult it became with each year that passed.

"I'm sorry," Destiny said, and then grew silent.

"It's okay. The years we had together were pretty terrific." He finished off his wine, and then asked. "What about you and your parents?"

"Just me and Mom. My dad passed shortly after my brother."

"Sorry," he said, frowning.

She shook her head and gave a half laugh. "Boy, are we two pathetic people or what?"

He laughed. "It certainly sounds that way." And for no reason at all, Miles found his thoughts drifting toward his coming birthday. He could almost hear the loud ticking of the clock. He didn't have much time left.

"Hello, hello?" Destiny snapped her fingers.

Miles blinked, and then apologized for his wandering brain.

"It's okay. I was just asking you what made you want to become a lawyer?"

"Money," he answered honestly. "Problem is that you don't learn until after graduation how much of a joke that notion is."

Destiny held up her glass. "Amen."

"What about you?"

Destiny tucked her legs under her. "I don't really think I had a choice in the matter. Lady Justice has bewitched just about everyone in my family for generations. To this day, my mother swears my first word was *objection* instead of *mommy*."

Miles laughed. "For some reason, I don't doubt that."

Her laugh deepened. "I don't, either."

Soon their laughter faded and both parties fell into their own private thoughts before Miles looked up and asked, "Any regrets?"

She drew in a deep breath and met his leveled gaze. "Plenty." At his surprised stare, she went on. "As you know, this isn't the easiest job in the world. A lot of times you get attached to the people you represent—you believe their stories of innocence and, more times than not, you end up being played a fool. Then there are cases where you don't know how you can stand to look at yourself in the mirror because you're defending someone you're convinced is guilty. And let's not discuss the problems with venality throughout the courts in recent years." She paused and shook her head. "But every once in a while, you stumble over a case that validates all that you believe in and forces you to step up to the plate. If you're up to the challenge, you deliver a home run." She shrugged as if she had trouble making sense of her own words.

"I can definitely relate," he said, but wondered at what had happened to inspire such an interesting soliloquy.

Destiny crossed her arms and remained reflective. "I had this one case where every fiber of my being screamed that my client wasn't a murderer. I fought like hell to save him, but…"

She closed her eyes and Miles was surprised by her strug-

gle for control of her emotions. The anguish in her expression
touched something within him and still he didn't know what
to say. Answers like "We all have to deal with such cases" or
"Hey, don't let the job get you down" seemed too crass and
unsympathetic. So instead, he said nothing.

"I don't know. Maybe I need to take a break. I've yet to
take a vacation since I've been with Phillips, Anderson and
Brown."

"You've got to be kidding me," he said, astonished.

"I wish I was." She shrugged again and emitted a low
laugh. "What can I say? I'm your typical workaholic."

"Workaholic?" He held his fingers up in shape of a cross
and shuddered. "Sounds like a horrible disease. It's not con-
tagious, is it?"

Destiny laughed. "I think you're safe. Besides, you have
quite a level of discipline yourself."

Perplexed, he asked, "Me?"

"Yes, you. What are you—some kind of health freak?"
She laughed, but noticed that he didn't.

"What?" she asked baffled. When he didn't readily respond, she laughed. "You are, aren't you?"

He shrugged and tried not to laugh at her amused expression. "Well, let's just say it's a long story."

"Like you said earlier, I'm not about to go anywhere any-
time soon."

Miles shook his head. "You'll laugh."

"Probably—but try me anyway."

He hesitated. The last thing he needed was for someone
else telling him how silly it was to believe in curses. He
drained what was left in his glass and looked at her. "Odds
are, I don't have much time left to live."

A long silence stretched between them before Destiny
reared her head back and released a hearty laugh.

Miles rolled his eyes. "I told you you would laugh."

Destiny couldn't respond. She was too busy wiping her eyes and trying to catch her breath.

Miles clenched his jaw and regretted his confession. Hell, he wasn't quite sure why he told her.

"So, is this the story you tell your girlfriends, the old 'make love to me because I only have six months to live' routine?"

Insulted, he snapped, "No."

It took a moment for her laughter to die, but when it did, she paused and studied him. "You're serious, aren't you?"

"Yes," he said, maintaining eye contact. He then watched a sudden cloud of concern come over her.

"Are you sick?"

His uneasiness ebbed away as he read genuine interest in her face. "No. I'm not sick, per se."

Concern morphed into doubt again. "If you're not sick then how to you know that you're going to die? You haven't been calling Warwick's Psychic Hotline, have you?"

He smiled. "Let's just say that it's a family curse."

"A curse?"

"For seven generations no man in my family has lived to see his forty-six birthday. And on Wednesday, I'll turn forty."

She said nothing as he watched her teeter on whether to believe him.

"I don't know what to say," she said guilelessly. "Are you sure? Well, of course you're sure, but…"

He nodded. "Don't get me wrong. There are people, like my mother, who think the curse is utter nonsense, but it's hard to overlook the facts."

"Seven generations?"

"That I'm aware of."

She shook her head, seeming to be fascinated. "What do they do—just drop dead on their forty-fifth birthday?" When he flinched, she added apologetically, "I mean, is it a case of heart problems or something like that?"

"Most of them were heart-related problems—but my father died in a car accident a week before turning forty-six."

"No," she drew back in a startled surprised.

"I know it sounds weird to believe in such things in this day and age, but it's hard to put a label like 'coincidence' on something like this."

She fell silent again with her reservations clearly written in her expression. But he was used to getting that reaction from most of his friends.

"It's got to be hard for you," she finally said, lost in thought. "I mean, it's one thing to go through life with everything being unknown, trying to find one's purpose or searching for your soul mate, but to go through all that with an expected time limit…" She shook her head. "Knowing something like that would drive most people crazy."

"I don't know about that." He shrugged. "My take on it is that I have to get as much life in as I possibly can. I try to enjoy and appreciate each day as it comes. It's not always easy, especially lately," he said, frowning.

He piqued her curiosity. "What's changed recently?"

"The number *forty*," he answered in a low tone. He paused and looked down at his empty glass. "It has such a final ring to it."

She covered his hand that lay on the arm of the sofa. "You could be wrong about this, you know."

His gaze lowered to her delicate hand and its warmth surprised and comforted him. "I've considered it. My father told me once not to put too much stock in curses." His chest tightened at the memory.

"He didn't believe in the curse?"

Miles shook his head. "For a time he actually had me convinced."

She squeezed his hand.

Miles slid his hand from beneath hers. "Can I get you something else to drink?"

The lights flickered on and suddenly the room was flooded with light.

Destiny smiled awkwardly. "No, thanks. I think I've had enough." She stretched lazily as Miles stood and reached for her empty glass.

"It's getting late. What time is it?" she asked.

He glanced at his watch and was startled to see just how right she was. "Four-thirty."

"A.M.?"

He smiled. "And you thought that you would never spend the night with me. Ha!"

She rolled her eyes. "You're incorrigible." She unfolded herself from the wing chair and cringed slightly at the sound of her joints popping. "I'm sure someone has to be working the front desk by now."

"Yeah. George usually works the graveyard shift. We probably could have called a few hours ago to get a key."

She nodded and covered her mouth as she yawned.

Miles placed the dishes in the dishwasher while Destiny used the phone. His eyelids grew heavy as he experienced a hefty dose of drowsiness. When he returned to the living room, she informed him that George was on his way up.

"Turns out there was a bad accident that damaged an electrical pole not too far from here," she said. "I didn't bother to ask George about Wendell. I don't want to get the boy in any kind of trouble."

Miles simply smiled. "Well," he said. "I hate to see this pleasant evening come to an end."

She smiled. "It was pleasant, wasn't it?"

He nodded. "I hate that it took so long to get to know each another. I can always use a good friend."

"Me, too," she affirmed with a smile.

The doorbell rang. Miles and Destiny started at its sudden sound.

"My, that was fast," Miles commented, heading toward the door.

George, an elderly black gentleman with twinkling eyes and a florescent white smile, greeted him on the other side of the door. "Good morning, Mr. Stafford. Ms. Brockman asked for me to deliver a spare key to her apartment here." He tilted up on his toes to dart a glance over Miles's shoulder. When he lowered his weight back onto the balls of his feet, he winked knowingly at Miles and handed over the key. "I hope the night's events haven't been too much of an inconvenience for either of you."

Miles shook his head as one side of his mouth lifted into a sly smile. "It was no trouble at all." He dug into his pocket, handed George a small tip along with a conspiratorial wink before closing the door.

"What's so amusing?" Destiny asked him as he returned to the living room still wearing a smile.

"Nothing," he responded with his voice laced with undeniable humor.

Her expression wrinkled with disbelief, but she didn't bother to interrogate him further. "Please tell me that was George at the door."

Miles held up the key. *"Pour vous, Mademoiselle."*

Her face flashed with instant relief. "Well, thank goodness." She walked over to him and held out her hand.

Miles dropped the copper key into her palm. "Shall I walk you to your door?"

She tilted her head in kind. "That's awfully chivalrous of you."

"Let's just say that it's one of my many good qualities." He made a dramatic bow.

"I don't know about 'many,' but yes you can walk me across the hall if you like."

"I like, I like," he said with a burst of alacrity. He gestured for her to take the lead and then followed close behind as they left his apartment.

A minute later, Destiny slipped the key into her door and turned the lock. When the door opened, she turned back to face Miles and was startled to find him standing so close.

"Oh," she said, stepping back into the partially open door. "Well, it has been quite an evening."

"Yes, it has. I hope we can do it again some time," he said thickly.

She swallowed, suddenly jittery from the intensity of his gaze. His hazel eyes, as well as the long curly lashes that surrounded them, had always fascinated her.

"Well…good night." She stepped back again and crossed the threshold into her apartment.

Miles again stepped forward. This time, he took hold of her hand and brought it up to his lips, and gave it a feathery kiss. "Good night, Desi."

She blinked at the nickname. Her hand—her whole arm— grew warm. And her jittering nerves had transformed into a swarm of butterflies batting madly throughout her body.

Miles's lips twitched into a smile, and then he turned and walked away.

Rooted by her door, she watched him cross over to his apartment, but managed, thankfully, to snap out of her reverie in time to close her door before he caught her gaping at him. But even then, she stood staring at the back of the door wondering what in hell had just happened.

Chapter 11

Lost in Miles's sinewy arms, Destiny melted at the exquisite feel of his lips pressed against her breasts. Desire consumed her and she couldn't get enough of his magic hands and glorious mouth. She moaned wantonly and arched her back in a silent invitation.

Everything about him was rock-hard and a throbbing ache pulsed in the center of her being. She gasped when his tongue slid expertly into her and she thrashed in shameful abandonment.

She murmured his name as heat swelled inside her. She thrashed her head against the pillow. Soon she begged for the sweet explosion that was just out of her reach.

Destiny's alarm clock blared and she bolted straight up in bed and looked around. It was a dream—but it had seemed so real. She fell back against the pillows and waited for her heartbeat to return to normal as she stared up at the ceiling.

Soon her thoughts returned to her evening with Miles. She

thought about his family curse. She wasn't sure if she believed in curses, but apparently Miles believed in his.

She rolled onto her side and caught the first rays of daylight peeping through the venetian blinds. She admired Miles's dedication to live each day to the fullest. It was a lot better than moping around and complaining about things she couldn't fix.

Miles was convinced he had less than six years to live. Who's to say that she didn't have less?

"If you hate your life so much then get up and do something to change it." Lu Jin's solution filled her head again.

Destiny sat up, a geyser of inspiration erupted inside of her. Why couldn't she take time to find out what she really wanted?

Then, as if in answer, Adam's image floated to the front of her mind and her heart dropped guiltily to the pit of her stomach. She closed her eyes in shame.

A part of her knew it wasn't feasible to try and live her brother's life, but it was so hard to let him go—even now. Miserable, she climbed out from beneath the comforter and walked over to the window to view the city.

At the sight of so many cars on the road, she wondered where everyone was going this early on a Saturday morning. Then again, it seemed everyone was in a hurry to get somewhere nowadays—herself included. She thought of her mother and admired that she'd acquired a new set of friends and had started traveling around the world. Of the two of them, Destiny was the only one still living in the past.

She drew in a deep, ragged breath, hoping it would help clear her head. It didn't. She wanted to talk with Miles again. She wondered at how he'd achieved the inner peace he exuded when facing such a doomed future and she wondered if she could achieve such a thing for herself.

* * *

Despite being tired as hell, Miles couldn't sleep. His mind kept drifting back over the evening he'd shared with Destiny. He would have never imagined that she was capable of such warmth and sincerity. He opened his eyes and stared up at the ceiling as he thought about the first time he'd ever met Destiny. He remembered thinking how beautiful she was. She was still beautiful, both inside and out.

Five years ago, I didn't appreciate her inner qualities; I was just interested in getting her into bed. Now? He shrugged in the dark. *Now, I do appreciate them.*

Problem was he didn't know what had happened between then and now to change his attitude. Destiny's face came into focus. When she talked about her brother or father, she appeared fragile, which up until last night, was never a word he'd use to describe Destiny Brockman.

He sat up in bed and leaned back against the headboard. For as long as he'd known Destiny, he'd thought of her as a fierce and dedicated attorney. Now he was aware there were more layers to her personality.

"One should never assume," he said out loud. He thought how she responded to his admission of a family curse. Well, after she'd stopped laughing anyway. The point was that she *did* stop.

He remembered what she'd said: "It's one thing to go through life with everything being unknown, trying to find one's purpose or searching for your soul mate, but to go through all that with an expected time limit…"

Miles frowned. Truth was he'd never tried to search for a purpose or even considered looking for a soul mate, despite his mother's desire for him to do so. In fact, this was the first time he contemplated whether he'd wasted his life. What legacy was he going to leave behind to tell the world that he was here—another boy with an expected forty-five-year time limit?

He shook his head, determined not to do that, never to do that. But there were plenty of couples who decided not to have children. Maybe he *should* consider finding a mate to spend the rest of his life with—well, what was left of it anyway.

He deliberated it some more and for the first time, he actually warmed to the idea of marriage. He laughed. "Just wait until Mom hears this."

Lu Jin arrived up at Destiny's apartment around ten o'clock with a severe hangover, and then promptly passed out on her sofa a few minutes later.

Destiny, on the other hand, dressed in a pair of rarely used sweat clothes. Today was the day she was going to change her life and the first thing she wanted to tackle was establishing a good workout regime. She left her friend passed out on the sofa, but was surprised to see Miles stepping out of his apartment also dressed in his jogging gear.

"I would have thought that you'd already completed your workout by this late hour," she said, smiling and locking her door.

"I would have, but I had this one woman over that kept me up all night. Guess I haven't lost my touch, huh?"

Embarrassed by the implication, Destiny's face warmed.

"Loosen up, I was just playing." He winked and locked his door. "So, what's this?" he asked, turning back toward her. "You're taking up running now?"

She shrugged. "Can't see how it could hurt."

"Did I inspire you?"

"A little. Not to mention those stairs last night nearly killed me."

He laughed. "So, how about you take a run with me? I'll go easy on you if you like."

"You would have to go *real* easy."

"I think I can handle that." He winked.

Twenty minutes later, Destiny gave serious thought to hailing a taxi for her aching and cramping body. As she jogged next to Miles through the park, she wasn't even sure if she was still breathing correctly. All she knew was that exercising was proving to be hazardous to her health.

Miles looked over at her, frowned and then led her over to a bench.

Destiny collapsed on the iron seat and heaved in big gulps of air.

"Are you going to be all right?" he asked with genuine concern.

She nodded, but still struggled to get enough air into her lungs.

"Where is your water bottle?" he asked.

She looked up perplexed.

"You didn't bring a water bottle?" He shook his head and reached for the bottle at his hip. "Here, drink some of this before you pass out."

Destiny greedily accepted the bottle and downed most of its contents in one gulp.

Miles laughed. "Take it easy."

Feeling somewhat refreshed, she handed the bottle back to him. "Thanks."

"Mind if I ask when was the last time you did this?"

"What—jogging?"

He nodded still smiling down at her.

"Well, actually, never." When his brows lifted in amusement, she went on to add, "Well, there's a first time for everything, right?"

"I suppose so. But maybe you're taking on too much on your first day. Perhaps we should walk back."

"You'll get no protest from me, but can we at least sit here a while until I catch my breath?"

"Sure, why not?" He chuckled and took the seat next to her.

Destiny finally gained control of her breathing and took a good look at her surroundings. The day was quite beautiful. The weather was not too hot nor too cool—perfect. The grass was a vibrant shade of green and the perennials were a swirl of colors.

"It's nice here," she said, admiringly. "I've lived in this city for most of my life and I don't remember ever coming here."

"I love it here," he said, nodding to a pair of joggers who passed by them.

"Friends of yours?" she inquired.

"Not really. We see each other running through here every once in a while. That's the best part about this place—the people."

Destiny nodded and turned her gaze back to her surroundings. She noticed a mother with her twins—maybe three years old—playing on a blanket beneath a large tree. A second later, a man joined them, carrying a picnic basket.

"They look happy," she commented without pulling her gaze from them.

"Yeah, they do."

The longing in his voice made her turn toward him and for one unguarded moment she saw sadness in his handsome features. Then it occurred to her that the family across from them represented something he didn't ever expect to experience—whether by choice or a predestined family curse.

She was suddenly at a loss for words.

"Are you ready to head back?" he asked in a hoarse whisper. His beautiful hazel eyes focused on her.

She nodded and swallowed a rising lump of emotions. "I hate that you didn't get your full run in today."

He waved her off as they stood. "Don't worry about it. I enjoyed your company much more." His eyes twinkled.

She smiled. "Boy, you really do know how to turn on the charm, don't you?"

He shrugged. "Hope you don't mind. Habits are hard to break."

Jabbing his arm with a light punch, she said, "I don't know what I'm going to do with you."

Lu Jin was just finished making a fresh pot of coffee when Destiny and Miles strolled playfully through the door. She swore it was a hallucination. She blinked, stared down at her coffee and then back up at the laughing couple.

"There's no way you're going to get that motion past Judge O'Brien." Destiny laughed. "She is one tough lady on the bench and you better walk in there with something more than charm to get your client off."

"So I've heard."

"Humph," Lu Jin cleared her throat.

Destiny and Miles turned.

"Anyone want to let me in on the joke?" she asked, lowering one hand to her hip.

"Well, I'm glad to see that you're back among the living," Destiny said, heading toward her and the kitchen.

"That remains to be seen." Lu Jin frowned when her friend walked past her.

Miles laughed, and then said, "I guess I better get going. I promised my mom I'd help her with some things around the house. Maybe we can catch up later."

"Are you sure I can't interest you in something to drink? I did, after all, rob you of your own water this morning."

He shook his head. "Nah. I think I can wait until I get across the hall." He walked to the door, and then called out over his shoulder, "Catch you later, Desi."

"Sure thing," she shouted back, and then moved over to the refrigerator.

Lu Jin watched the entire exchange with disbelief and furrowed brows. Slowly, she turned and waltzed back into the kitchen. "I think you've got some explaining to do." She sat her coffee mug down and crossed her arms.

"What do you mean?" Destiny pulled out a carton of milk, checked the expiration date and then sniffed the contents before rolling her eyes. "I swear this stuff goes bad the minute I put it in here."

Lu Jin's irritation rose and brought her even closer to sobriety. "I mean, what the hell is going on between you and Mr. Gigolo from across the hall?"

Destiny shrugged. "Nothing." She went over to the sink and poured out the milk.

"Nothing?" Lu Jin crossed her arms. "The last time I checked, you two couldn't stand to be in the same room together."

"Oh, that." Destiny shrugged again and then went back to the refrigerator. "I guess I was wrong about him."

Lu Jin waited for more information and when none came her irritation transformed into confusion. "That's it? You were wrong...after five years?"

"Pretty much." Destiny flittered about the kitchen as if they weren't talking about a man whom she'd called everything but a child of God since their first meeting.

"Okay. Who are you and what have you done with my best friend?"

Destiny laughed as she poured herself a tall glass of orange juice. "Okay. Maybe I do owe you an explanation."

"I'd say so."

"Let's see. Where do I start?"

"Start with whether you slept with him," Lu Jin said, pointedly.

"What?"

"Come on. We both know the man has more notches on his bedpost than Casanova."

"That's true," Destiny acquiesced with a nod of her head. "And the answer to your question is no. I didn't sleep with him."

"Damn." Lu Jin exhaled. "I was hoping to get the 4-1-1 on him."

Destiny slapped her friend's arm as she passed by to exit the kitchen. "I don't know what I'm going to do with you."

"Yeah, yeah." Lu Jin retrieved her coffee cup and followed Destiny all the way to her bedroom. "All right. We've established that you didn't sleep with him. So tell me what *did* happen."

"Well, let's see. Last night after you left, I broke up with Jefferson." She flashed Lu Jin her bare left hand.

"What?" Lu Jin sloshed coffee on herself, and then cursed a blue streak.

"You have the mouth of a sailor."

"So you keep reminding me. I can't believe you broke up with Jefferson. The man is perfect."

"He's a free man if you want him." Destiny shrugged at her friend's look of shock. "Come on, Lu Jin. The man was boring. His idea of a fun date is watching a twenty-four-hour marathon of tax laws on Court TV."

"But he's gorgeous."

Destiny rolled her eyes and proceeded to undress. "You're starting to sound like a broken record. I want a man with a few more attributes, if it's all the same with you."

"Like Mr. Magic Man from across the hall?"

"Mr. Magic Man, as you call him, has turned out to be…" She drew in a deep breath and reflected. "To be a deep person and a really nice guy. I'm glad we're finally friends."

Lu Jin frowned. "Are you sure you haven't slept with him?"

Destiny smiled and winked before turning toward the bathroom. "I'm going to take a shower."

"You better not be holding out on me," Lu Jin called after her.

With a mischievous laugh, Destiny closed the bathroom door, purposely leading Lu Jin to believe that something had indeed happened between her and Miles. And in some small way, something had.

Chapter 12

Violet took pride in knowing everything there was to know about her son and judging by the way he kept whistling while he worked on the bathroom pipes, she surmised something was going on. However, when she inquired into what had put Miles in such a good mood, he simply responded with a despondent shrug and said, "I'm just happy."

"This sudden spurt of happiness wouldn't happen to have been inspired by a lady, would it?" she asked, hopefully.

Miles laughed and disappeared once again beneath the sink.

It took everything Violet had to pretend that his withholding of information wasn't getting to her, but she suspected he knew that already. She wanted to call her friends and tell them her suspicion, but there was a high probability that she could be wrong about this—again.

Leaning against the frame of the bathroom door, Violet tackled their stalemate from a different angle.

"Did I tell you that Lila's daughter is getting married?"

"Oh?" he asked with a spark of interest. "Isn't Barbara her daughter?"

Violet hid a smile and crossed her arms. "Uh-huh."

He stopped what he was doing for a moment to say, "She's a nice girl. I'm sure she'll make her fiancé a very happy man," and resumed working.

Violet attempted to read in between the lines, but came up empty. "You know it's a shame that you two never hit it off. You both had a lot in common."

"I guess it just wasn't in the cards for us." He maneuvered around her interrogation. "Can you hand me the wrench?"

Violet rolled her eyes and bent down to hand him the wrench that was well within his reach. "I swear, Miles. I don't understand why you have to be so difficult."

He laughed again. "You're starting again," he said in a teasing voice. "You promised not to bug me about settling down or fixing me up on blind dates."

"I wouldn't have to start if you would just be reasonable. I don't want to fill the rest of my days watching you throw your life away. I want grandchildren and I want them now."

Miles pushed himself out from beneath the bathroom sink with neither a smile nor frown.

Violet didn't know what to make of his calmness. There was no real justification for her throwing such a tantrum, but as the years rolled by she was beginning to believe Miles's declaration of never settling down and giving her grandchildren.

"Are you finished now?" he asked, looking up at her.

Still unable to read anything in his expression, she drew in a deep breath and nodded.

Miles finally smiled. "Good." He got up from the floor and kissed her on the cheek. "I can't have my best girl storming around here all upset."

He walked out the bathroom, but not before she caught a glimpse of mischief in his eyes.

Suspicion crept over her again. Something was definitely up. She turned and followed him down to the kitchen where he retrieved a can of Coke. "You want one?" he asked, turning around to face her.

"You know perfectly well that I only buy those for you." She sat the kitchen counter.

Miles popped the tab and took a deep gulp from the can.

Violet studied him. "There's something different about you today and I'm going to hound you until you tell me what it is."

"Is that right?" he asked with yet another laugh.

"Yeah." She nodded. "So why don't you just save me some time and tell me what it is?"

He moved to the counter where she sat and leaned closer. "I don't know if you can handle what I'm going to say."

"You're engaged?" she asked, clasping her hands together. Hope bloomed in her heart and in her voice. At this point she didn't care to what or to whom he was engaged—it was a step in the right direction.

"Okay, maybe you can handle it," he said.

Violet jumped from her chair ready to dance a jig. "I'm right, aren't I?"

"Hold on, hold on. No, I'm not engaged."

"You're about to be engaged?" She guessed again.

"No, that's not it, either."

Hope took a nosedive into despair as she covered her heart with her hand. "Dear God, please don't tell me that you're about to shack up with some floozy." She reached for the stool again to sit down. "And she's probably knocked up. My grandchildren are going to be born out of wedlock."

"Whoa. Slow down. No one's pregnant and I'm not going to shack up with anyone, either. You really do have a low opinion of me."

"Oh, thank God." She propped her elbows up and lowered her head into her hands. "You gave me quite a scare there for a moment."

Miles frowned. "Wait a minute. Are you saying that you wouldn't love your grandchildren if they were born out of wedlock?"

She jerked her head up. After reading his expression, she slapped his hand. "Stop playing. Don't you know it's not nice to tease your mother like this?"

Still laughing, he pulled her into a quick hug. "I'm sorry. I just couldn't resist."

"Uh-huh." She pulled out of his embrace and waved a slender finger at him. "Don't think you've gotten off the hook. You still haven't told me what has you in such a good mood."

His laughter deepened. "I swear nothing gets by you."

"No, it doesn't. So cough it up. What's the good news?"

"The good news is that a friend of mine has finally showed me the error of my ways. Since time is ticking away and I'm not getting much younger—"

Violet pressed her fingers to her ears. "If this is going to be another speech about you dying, I don't want to hear it."

Miles gently pulled her hands away from her ears and said with a wide smile. "My good news is that I *want* to find the right girl and settle down."

Lu Jin didn't know what to make of Destiny when they went shopping. On a day she'd expected to watch her friend load up with more business suits, she was stunned when Destiny had instead gone into Victoria's Secret to carouse for lingerie.

"What do you think of this one?" Destiny held up a deep purple number that would have done Prince proud.

"Since when did you start wearing thongs?" she asked, frowning.

"Since now. I think it's time that I change my whole outlook on life." She turned and held up the same outfit, but in red. "Now this should turn a few heads, don't you think?"

"I don't know you anymore."

And on it went for two hours. In the end, Lu Jin guessed her friend had bought at least one item from every collection and in some cases two or three in different colors. Destiny then passed up the chance to shop in her favorite stores: Lord and Taylor and Neiman Marcus. Instead, she shopped in private boutiques where Destiny only tried on outfits that were very short and very tight.

"I think you lied to me," Lu Jin finally said, sitting on a small bench outside of the changing room and waiting to see what her friend would look like in yet another outfit.

"What do you mean?" Destiny's head jutted over the stall door.

Lu Jin shook her head determined not to buy her little innocent act any longer. "Something happened between you and Miles last night and you're holding out on me." She fell back against the wall and bumped her head. "Ouch, damn it."

Destiny's head disappeared behind the door. "Chill out, Lu Jin. Nothing happened."

"So what's with all this?"

"What's with all what?"

Lu Jin stood. "All of this—new clothes and sexy lingerie. This isn't exactly the behavior of a woman who just broke off her engagement."

Destiny stepped from behind the door in an eye-popping, black number that Lu Jin thought suited herself a lot more than her friend.

"So what do you think?" Destiny stretched out her hands and twirled in front of her friend.

"I hate it," Lu Jin said in a pout.

Destiny rolled her eyes and turned to face a mirror. "You do not. You're just being contrary."

"Okay, then. It doesn't suit you."

Destiny frowned, and then chewed her bottom lip as she assessed her appearance. She reached up and removed the clip from the nape of her neck and shook free her hair. "I don't know. I think I can work with this."

Lu Jin sighed.

Destiny smiled and caught her friend's gaze through the mirror. "I thought that you'd be happy that I finally got out of the house and started doing something."

"I would be even happier if you started acting like yourself and not like me. It's eerie."

Destiny turned. "You want to know what happened last night?"

Lu Jin's frown curved the opposite way. "Finally. The truth."

"Last night while I sat talking to Miles in his darkened apartment, I had an epiphany."

"Layman terms, please."

"Talking to Miles made me realize what I've been doing wrong with my life. He made me realize that I needed to seize the day—to try and live life to the fullest because tomorrow isn't promised to anyone."

Lu Jin stared at her. "Did you fall and bump your head?"

Destiny slapped her open palm against her forehead as she walked past Lu Jin to return to the dressing room. "I know it sounds crazy," she said through the door.

"Yeah, a little." She turned. "In one night, this man you couldn't stand for five years has convinced you to stop being yourself and start doing God knows what."

Destiny's head appeared over the stall. "That's just it, Lu Jin. I haven't been acting like myself. I've been trying to live a lie. I've been so busy trying to do things I thought Adam would or be the person he wanted to be that I had long stopped being myself."

Lu Jin stopped frowning and Destiny, once again, disappeared behind the stall.

"And do you want to know what the sad part is?" Destiny asked.

"What?"

Destiny opened the door. Now dressed back in her clothes. "I don't know who I am. I don't know what I want to be. That's the real reason I broke up with Jefferson—and that's why I'm going to quit my job."

"You're quitting?"

Destiny nodded. "I have to. It's smothering me."

Lu Jin drew in a deep breath and just stared at her friend. "I had no idea that you were so miserable. I thought that you were just going through a phase, or suffering through some early midlife crisis."

Destiny waved off the distress that was creeping into her friend's expression. "I did, too, until last night."

"Oh, I feel awful. I should have been there for you last night." She opened her arms and Destiny accepted her embrace.

"But you did help me. There is no need for you to feel bad. You're my best friend. I know that I can always count on you. You're my rock." Destiny pulled away, smiling.

"How did I help?"

"You told me if I hated my life so much then to get up and do something to change it. And that's exactly what I'm doing."

"Yeah?" Lu Jin smiled and wiped the tears from the corners of her eyes.

"Yeah," Destiny reemphasized. "And it was the best advice I could have gotten," she said, smiling.

"I can't believe I'm blubbering like this." Lu Jin's smile wobbled as she continued to mop her face dry.

"Yeah. You better quit it if you don't want anyone else to know how much of an old softy you are."

Lu Jin laughed. "Good point. I do have a reputation to protect."

"So, are you up for some more shopping?"

"Bring it on, baby."

Chapter 13

Miles woke up Wednesday with a deep sense of dread and foreboding, mainly because it was his fortieth birthday. But he pushed himself out of bed determined to shake off those bad feelings. After brushing his teeth and splashing water onto his face, he donned his running clothes and rushed out of the apartment.

"You're five minutes late, Birthday Boy," Destiny said, tapping the face of her wristwatch. In a stylish workout suit, she looked more prepared to strut down a fashion runway than to tackle a two-mile run.

Miles shook his head. "How many outfits did you buy on your shopping spree this past weekend?" He locked his door, and then turned back to face her.

She shrugged. "A few." She moved over to him and removed a large, but thin, square package from behind her back. "Happy birthday."

Surprised, his eyes darted from the box's sky-blue wrapping back up to her smiling face. "You really shouldn't have."

"I know, but I did, so open it."

He hesitated and then tore into the box. He laughed when he pulled out an old Miles Davis album.

"The other morning when we went jogging you said you didn't have this one."

"Where did you find this? I've looked everywhere for this album."

"Actually, my brother loved him. I'm sure he wouldn't mind my passing this on to another fan."

Touched, he didn't quite know what to say. "I'm not sure if I should accept this," he said honestly.

She held up her hands, refusing to take it back. "It's yours. Besides, for the last seven years it has done nothing but collect dust in my place."

He smiled again, and then leaned down to kiss her tenderly on the cheek. He caught the subtle scent of roses from her hair and her skin. "Thank you," he said. He turned and reentered his apartment to put away the album.

When he returned, they headed toward the elevator bay.

"You know the point of working out is for the exercise— not to try and pick up guys while jogging through the park." He brought the conversation back to his early comment about her clothes as he pressed the down button.

"Uh-huh." She crossed her arms as her lips twisted into a sarcastic frown. "How many women have you met over the years during your morning runs?"

Amusement curled the corners of his lips before he had a chance to stop it.

"My point exactly," she said, not waiting for a response.

The elevator arrived and they stepped inside together.

"Well, I have to admit that I'm impressed. This is your

My Destiny

fifth day in a row running with me. After that first one, I assumed you'd give up."

"I don't quit too many things."

"Just your job and your engagement?"

She laughed. "Something like that."

Their run through the park was nice and Destiny smiled at the small community of joggers. She knew no one's name, but nodded her greetings to familiar faces as she passed them. She no longer had difficulty breathing, but she appreciated Miles cutting his usual four-mile run down to two until she built up her endurance level.

"So now that you're not working for Phillips, Anderson and Brown, do you have any idea what you're going to do next?" Miles asked her out of the blue.

"Not really. I thought a lot about taking a year off and doing some traveling or even going back to school."

"Back to school?"

"It's just an idea."

"For the record, I think you're making a big mistake," he said as they rounded yet another curve on the narrow trail.

"Why?"

"Because you're one hell of a lawyer." When she said nothing to this, he went on. "I know you've been on some kind of mission to complete the things you think your brother had set out to do, but have you ever thought that maybe this life or career was meant for you all along?"

Destiny frowned as she looked over at him. "What do you mean?"

He shrugged. "By your own admission, every member of your family had careers in law. Your mother was even a paralegal at one time, right?"

"Yeah, so?"

"So. Maybe you haven't been trying to fill your brother's ambition, but were simply following your own."

Destiny frowned as she mulled over Miles's words. They were definitely food for thought. After ten minutes of silence had passed, she glanced at him again. "Were you always so insightful?"

"Yeah, but don't tell anybody."

She laughed. "I'll carry it to my grave."

"You know, you've been a lot of help for me, as well."

"I have?" she asked, astonished.

"Yeah. I thought a lot about searching for that mysterious soul mate you were talking about the other night."

"You've got to be kidding. You're actually going to settle down, have two-point-five children and buy a dog?"

It was his turn to laugh. "Something like that." He returned her earlier flippant response. "I've even made it official by telling my mom."

She stopped laughing and emitted a low whistle. "That does make it official," she agreed. "But I don't remember saying *I* believe in soul mates. I just said that other people search for things like that."

"You don't?"

"No."

"Then why did you break your engagement to Jefferson?"

"Because we're not that well suited."

Miles slowed down.

"What?" She stopped and waited for him to catch back up with her.

"You're lying, that's what. You and Jefferson had more in common than you're letting on. Trust me. I know the man. You want to know what I think?"

"Do I have a choice?"

"I think you broke up with him because you do believe that there's someone better for you out there. Maybe you like the idea of a knight in shining armor riding up and rescuing you."

"For your information, I don't need rescuing." She started

jogging again. "And yes, I broke up with Jefferson because I thought that there had to be something out there that's better for me, but that doesn't mean I believe there's a *perfect* someone for me, just a better one."

Miles frowned beneath the weight of her stare. "So you think I'm overshooting it with looking for a quote-unquote soul mate?"

"Why don't you start off with baby steps and actually go on two consecutive dates," she answered with a sarcastic smile.

He grimaced at the thought. "You know this may be harder than I originally thought."

"You're hopeless," she said, shaking her head. She removed the bottle of water from her hip and began to drink greedily from it.

"You know what, Destiny? I think you're the first attractive woman I don't want to sleep with," Miles proclaimed. His voice filled with a certain measure of awe.

Destiny nearly choked. "That's good to know."

"No. I mean it. In the last two weeks I haven't been tempted once to make a pass at you."

"You made a pass at me yesterday."

"We were joking around. I mean a real pass—one I fully expect you to take me up on."

"Oh. I'm glad you cleared that up."

"Come on. I'm being for real. I've never had a real woman friend before. This is a step toward maturity for me."

Destiny laughed and shook her head as she returned the water bottle to her hip. "Well, I'm real happy for you."

"What about you?" he asked.

"What about me? I took the plunge into maturity a long time ago. I have plenty of male friends."

"Sure you do."

"What? I really do."

"Are these guy friends of yours single?"

She shrugged. "Yeah, so?"

"So, I'm willing to bet you put them in that friend zone against their wills. Every one of them is just waiting for the opportunity to be something more to you, even if it's just for one night."

"You know I'm amazed that your head isn't more pointed because you really do have a narrow mind."

"I'm just being honest."

"That's what's scaring me."

"I'm telling you how a man thinks, that's all. It's very rare for a man not to want to sleep with every woman he sees."

"Are you telling me that at one time you wanted to sleep with me?"

"The minute I laid eyes on you."

Her head jerked in his direction, astonishment seized her features. "You're kidding."

"Please. In my mind's eye, I had you stripped and lying beneath me before I ever bothered helping you with that box." He smiled at her shocked and reddened face. "Come on. You've got to know that you got a cute little figure there."

"I think we should change the subject."

"Why? It's just starting to get interesting." When she said nothing, he couldn't help but ask, "How about you?"

"How about me what?"

"What did you think of me?"

"I'm not answering that."

Miles enjoyed her deepening coloring. "Come on. You can tell me."

"There's nothing to tell."

"You wanted to jump my bones, didn't you?"

"That's a lie," she said with a little too much force.

"Uh-huh," he said, unconvinced. "If you say so."

"You know in the past week, I've forgotten how big your ego inflates."

"Can it be that you use sarcasm to hide a deeper feeling?" He watched as her jawline hardened and he laughed. "All right. All right. I'll stop. I was just trying to give you a hard time."

"And you're doing a damn good job of it, too."

"You're way too easy to embarrass. You need to try and loosen up a bit."

"Why? Do you think I'm a prude or something?"

"No. Well, not anymore."

Destiny frowned. "So, you mean at one time you thought I was."

"Well…it was kind of hard not to." He winced. The last thing he wanted to do was hurt her feelings and judging by the look on her face that was exactly what he was doing. "But hey, this was all before you had your mini breakdown last week." He grimaced. Now he'd managed to successfully jam both feet into his mouth.

She glared over at him. "My, don't you have a way with words?"

"Sorry," he said, and meant it.

She held his gaze for a brief moment, and then her features softened. "It's all right. You're right. Lu Jin has been calling me a prude since college. I don't know, maybe I do need to learn how to loosen up." She focused her attention back onto the trail. "You know, you both have a lot of similar qualities. Maybe I should try and fix you two up." An image of them together caused a sour taste to pool in her mouth.

Miles laughed. "You forget I've met Lu Jin."

"What? You don't find her attractive?" she asked with perhaps a trace of hope in her voice, but he disappointed her with his next statement.

"Are you kidding? A man would have to be blind or dead not to find her attractive—and I'm neither. But one of the main rules for a player is not to date another player. It's a bad mix."

"I have a feeling I should be writing all this stuff down," she said.

"If you're about to jump back into the dating scene, then maybe that's not such a bad idea. You know I could teach you all the games to look out for."

"Okay, then, I'll bite. Why is it bad for a player to date another player?"

"I don't think that you're going to like my answer to that question."

"That's okay. I haven't liked most of what you've said."

Miles laughed. "Well, it's kind of like how a man looks at infidelity. He can lie to himself as to why he does it or why it's okay, but he could never forgive his girl if she does it. That's pretty much what a female player is all about. She's bouncing from one guy to the next for one reason or another. And the coolest brother out there can't handle that."

"Sexism at its best," Destiny replied with disdain. "I can't believe you actually think like this."

"Hey, I'm not the only one."

She shook her head.

"I told you you weren't going to like my answer."

"I'll never doubt you again."

They jogged out of the park and within a few minutes Destiny spotted their high-rise looming before them.

"You know the good thing about all of this is we're the exception to the rule," Miles said suddenly.

"What do you mean?"

"It's like I've said before—you're the first attractive woman I don't want to sleep with. And you've admitted that you're not attracted to me—so we're free to have the perfect female-male friendship, right?"

"Right," she agreed, not bothering to correct him on the fact that she'd never said that she wasn't attracted to him— far from it.

Chapter 14

"What do you mean you're not interested in sleeping with her?" Wes asked incredulously. "Are you coming down with something?"

Miles laughed as he picked up his poker hand. "I feel fine. Destiny and I are just friends."

Wes shifted his gaze from Theo and Juan. "Are you two hearing this? He and his *sexy* neighbor are just friends."

Theo removed the fat Cuban cigar from his mouth and blew out a thick cloud of smoke. "I hear him, but I don't believe it."

"Comments like that can get a man's player card taken away," Juan added with a sly grin.

"I know damn well that you undergraduates aren't trying to school me about the rules of the game." Miles's chest puffed up with indignity, but his eyes twinkled with amusement.

"Nah, nah," Theo said, returning the cigar to the corner of his mouth. "We ain't trying to school ya or nothing, but you are talking a little crazy. Every brother knows that a man can't be friends with a woman, especially with a fine sister like the one living across the hall."

"Exactly my point," Wes agreed, and then rewarded Theo with a jive hand slap.

Miles only rolled his eyes. "That's a bunch of bull. Destiny and I are two mature adults having a mature, *nonsexual* relationship."

"What you and Destiny are doing is fooling yourselves," Wes corrected. "Have you ever seen that chick flick, *When Harry Met Sally?*"

"I must have missed it," Miles said. "Is anybody going to open the bid?"

"I'll open with five," Juan said.

"I'll call," Wes said, and then returned his attention to Miles. "Anyway, the movie's premise was whether a man and a woman could really be friends without sex becoming an issue."

Miles's brows rose in mild interest. "Is that right?"

"Yeah. In the beginning Billy Crystal's character is convinced that the whole man/woman friendship can't exist without the sex ruining everything."

"Who's Billy Crystal?" Juan asked, propping his elbows on the table.

"He's the short, funny guy in *City Slickers,*" Theo answered with a smile.

"Do you two mind?" Wes asked, annoyed.

"Sorry," Theo and Juan apologized in unison.

"Like I was saying, the movie spans through all of this mushy stuff just to prove Crystal's point. Somewhere in the middle, while they were lying to themselves and calling each other 'friends,' sex happens and changes everything. Suddenly, the blonde chick wanted more from the relationship and by the end of the movie, they were married."

"But Destiny and I aren't having sex."

Wes, Theo and Juan laughed.

"What you mean to say is you and Destiny aren't having sex *yet*," Wes corrected.

Miles frowned. "That was only a movie."

The guys laughed again.

"Art imitates life all the time, my friend."

There was a knock on the door and Miles placed his card hand facedown onto the table. "I still say you guys are wrong." He stood and shook his head at his friend's laughter. "You'll see," he said, heading toward the door.

When he pulled it open, his face exploded into a wider smile at the sight of his friends, Jared and Kyle. "So you two were finally able to get away from the old balls and chains?"

"Ha. Ha. Ha." Kyle smirked, and then held up a case of beer. "I'm bearing gifts, so let me in."

Miles stepped back and allowed the brothers to enter.

"Well, it's about time," Wes hollered. "Now we can get this game going."

"Who's winning?" Jared asked, removing his leather jacket.

"Who else?" Everyone else at the table responded with equal sarcasm.

Miles held his hands up high into the air. "Don't hate the player—hate the game."

A wave of popcorn flew in his direction.

"Hey, hey, you guys, watch it. The last time we played here ya'll trashed my place and left me to clean up everything."

"Who are you kidding?" Wes griped. "We all know you have a maid service in here twice a week."

Miles returned to his seat and threw a kernel of popcorn at Wes. "Yes, but they always charge extra after poker night."

"Boo hoo. Now, how many cards do you want?"

Miles took another look at his hand and removed a five and eight of clubs. "Give me two." He looked over at Jared.

"So what's been up with you, man? You haven't joined us in a while."

Jared shrugged, and then bummed a cigar from Theo. "Just trying to hang in there until Kimberly has that baby."

"Ya'll ain't had that baby yet?" Wes frowned, taking two cards for himself and wincing slightly when he looked at his new cards. "I fold."

"Nay, but junior's due here any minute."

"So what in the hell are you doing here tonight?"

"I had to get the hell out of Dodge. Kimberly's two sisters and mother are here and they are driving me crazy with honey do's."

Theo shook his head and tossed down his cards. "This is too rich for my blood. I fold, too." He then looked at Jared. "What the heck are honeydews?"

All the men in the room responded in unison. "Honey, can you *do* this, and honey, can you *do* that?" The guys looked at each other and burst out in a chorus of laughter.

"I can't believe we're actually about to have a sleepover," Lu Jin said, filling a plastic bowl with freshly popped popcorn.

"Hey, this is going to be fun." Destiny loaded a tray with soft drinks. "It'll feel like we're back in college."

They were dressed in flannel nightgowns and Lu Jin had her hair pulled back in a hair band. Destiny's hair was parted down the center and brushed into two pigtails.

When the doorbell rang, Destiny bubbled with excitement. "I got it." She flashed Lu Jin a quick smile, and then rushed out of the kitchen. "This is going to be so much fun," she said to herself before flinging open the door and releasing a squeal of delight at the sight of her two old college friends: Debra and Monique.

Lu Jin shot from around the corner and also screamed.

The four women fell into a large group hug in the doorway, their shrieks echoing throughout the hall.

They broke apart when the door across the hall suddenly flew open and Miles filled the door frame.

"Sorry," Destiny gushed. "I guess we got a little carried away."

A rumble of men's laughter spilled out into the hall.

"No problem." Miles jerked his thumb over his shoulder to indicate the crowd behind him. "Poker night."

Destiny nodded. "Slumber party."

Miles quirked a brow while an amused grin lifted the corners of his mouth. "At least that explains the outfit."

Destiny looked down at her nightgown, and then flushed when she looked back up at him.

"Don't worry. A lot of guys find flannel sexy." He winked, and then nodded at her friends. "Have a good night, ladies," he said, and then disappeared behind the door.

Debra and Monique turned open-mouthed toward Destiny and Lu Jin.

"Come on in, before we disturb anyone else," Destiny said, gesturing them in.

"Who on earth is that fine brotha?" Monique finally managed to ask when Destiny closed the door behind them.

Destiny shrugged. "Oh, that's Miles. Don't worry, he's harmless."

"I think I've died and gone to heaven. That man has the prettiest eyes I've ever seen," Debra gushed, fanning herself with her hands. "It should be against the law to look that good."

"I heard *that*," Monique agreed and high-fived Debra.

Destiny laughed. "Then I should warn you, Miles Stafford is quite the ladies' man."

"I can testify to that," Lu Jin agreed, and disappeared into the kitchen. A few seconds later, she reemerged carrying two large bowls of popcorn. "I don't think I've ever seen him with the same woman twice."

Monique placed a hand over her heart. "Hell, once would do me just fine."

The women laughed.

"If I didn't know any better, I'd say Mr. Harmless was checking you out," Debra said, placing her hand on her hip and eyeing Destiny.

"Please." Destiny waved off the comment.

"Uh-huh. 'A lot of guys find flannel sexy,'" Monique mimicked Miles.

"Lu Jin, will you tell them nothing's going on between me and Miles?"

Lu Jin shook her head and joined in on the women's laughter. "Actually, I'm on their side. There was definitely something to his comment."

Destiny rolled her eyes and went into the kitchen to retrieve some of the refreshments. When she returned, she saw that her friends hadn't moved an inch; instead, they stood in a semicircle staring at her with their arms crossed.

"Drop the subject," Destiny warned, but for some reason was unable to control the smile hugging her lips.

The girls erupted with laughter and Destiny's embarrassment deepened.

"All right, spill it. We want details," Debra said.

"According to her there are no details," Lu Jin answered instead. "At least not yet." She wiggled her brows.

Destiny continued on to the living room. "Miles and I are friends. Period. End of story."

Monique frowned. "Why on earth would you want to keep a brotha like that in the friend category?"

"Because…" Destiny shrugged, not really having an answer.

"Uh-huh. Just what I thought. You're lying to yourself."

Lu Jin perked up with a mischievous grin. "You like him and you won't admit it."

"I do not. I just can't explain it to you. Miles and I don't see each other that way. We connect on a level that transcends anything I've experienced with another man."

That won another gust of laughter from the women.

Lu Jin approached her and draped an arm around her shoulders. "Transcends anything you've experienced with another man? You're not in the middle of a legal deposition here. We're your girls and we can see the obvious even if you can't."

Destiny shook her head and pulled away from Lu Jin. "You don't know what you're talking about." She set the tray of drinks down on the coffee table, and then stood with her hands settled against her hips. "I don't see what the big deal is. I've had plenty of friendships with men—take Zack and Elliott, for example."

"Both of them would cut off their right arm for a night with you and you know it," Lu Jin said in a matter-of-fact tone.

"Let you tell it, every man I meet wants to jump my bones." Destiny grew exasperated.

"Well," Debra cut in. "Remember Victor and Andre from school."

"Yeah." Monique snapped her fingers, and then turned back toward Destiny. "They used to follow you around like puppies."

"And so did Alfonso and Benjamin."

Destiny looked at the small group, frowning. "They did not follow me around like puppies."

"They did, but you were too busy with your studies to even notice," Lu Jin said. Her smile broadened as Destiny's faded. "In my humble opinion, there isn't a woman alive who has male friends who, at one time or another, didn't want to have sex with her." She turned to Monique and Debra. "Am I right?"

Monique rewarded her with another high five.

Debra hesitated. "I don't know about that."

Destiny moved over to stand next to Debra. "What it is is crap." She cast a withering glance over at Lu Jin and Monique. "Just because Lu Jin's hormones are turned on to full blast and she believes that every man she sees wants to bed her doesn't make it so."

Lu Jin's head reared back with a hearty laugh. "The difference between you and me is that I'm observant and more experienced."

"More experienced?" Destiny asked. "I would have used a different term, but whatever."

"Oooh," Debra and Monique responded in succession.

Lu Jin only laughed.

Destiny decided to change the subject. "Okay, you two. Why don't you go change into your pajamas while we finish putting out the snacks and getting the movie ready."

"Deal," Debra said, heading in the direction Destiny had pointed. "By the way, what movie are we watching?"

"A classic." Lu Jin wiggled her brows. *"When Harry Met Sally."*

"That's the woman you're worried Miles will succumb to and have a relationship with?" Theo asked Wes. "The one wearing the Pippi Longstocking hairdo?"

Another chorus of laughter rang from the table.

Miles smiled. "You guys need to behave. Destiny is a very attractive woman despite her evening apparel."

Wes leaned back in his chair while he nursed his beer bottle. "So you've noticed that she's attractive?"

"It's kind of hard not to." Miles shrugged and looked to Theo when he began to smirk. "Even when she's wearing floor-length flannel nightgowns and styling her hair like Pippi Longstocking."

Theo struggled not to laugh.

"And you're telling me you think you can honestly have a platonic relationship with a woman who you admit to finding attractive?" Wes pressed.

"Didn't we already have this conversation?" Miles looked around at his friends, all of whom were shaking their heads. "Just because you knuckleheads have never had a real friendship with a woman, doesn't mean that it's impossible."

"If my memory serves me correctly," Wes said with a broadening smile, "you've never had one, either."

Chapter 15

Adele entered The Prime restaurant and searched the crowd for a familiar face. After few minutes she caught sight of Violet waving frantically at a table near the back. She smiled and waved before maneuvering through a throng of people.

When she reached the table, Violet stood up and gave her a hug in greeting.

"You look absolutely wonderful. I'd say Bermuda agreed with you."

"Thanks. I had a wonderful time." Adele took her seat and laid her purse beside her friend's in a vacant chair. "Have you been waiting long?"

"Not really—about ten minutes. I went ahead and placed our drink orders with the waiter, though. You wanted a Chardonnay, right?"

"You know me so well," Adele responded in kind.

At that exact moment, the waiter appeared at their table and set the drinks down. "Are you ladies ready to order?"

"Can we have a few more minutes?" Adele asked, opening her menu.

"Certainly," the waiter assured her, and then scurried off to the next table.

Violet leaned over in her chair and said excitedly, "Well, I have some great news."

Adele's brows rose. "Well, let's hear it. I definitely can use some good news."

"Miles came over to the house the other day and you'll never guess what he told me."

"What?"

Violet placed a hand over her chest as if her heart were doing double time. "He's ready to settle down."

Adele's mouth fell open. "You've got to be kidding me. He actually said that?"

Violet nodded her head. "Yes. Can you believe it? He even asked me about Reverend Henderson's daughter, Camille. Unfortunately, she got married last summer. But can you believe it?"

"Not by what you've been telling me about him. No wonder you're practically glowing."

"More like flying. I'd almost given up on the matter and assumed that he would be the end of the Stafford family line. Now this. I can't tell you how excited I am."

Adele tried to share her friend's enthusiasm, but when her gaze lowered, her smile shifted a bit.

Violet leaned forward and covered her hand with her own. "Are you all right, Adele?"

Her gaze focused back on her friend as she waved off her concerns. "Oh, pay no attention to me. I'm happy for you. Really, I am. I know that this is the very thing you've been wishing for."

Violet's concerned gaze never left her friend's face. "Then what's troubling you?"

"Nothing," Adele lied, but when it became apparent that Violet wasn't buying it, she decided to tell her the truth. "Well, when I returned home, I was expecting to dive back into planning Destiny's wedding, but she called the wedding off."

"What?" Violet asked astonished.

"I know. Can you believe it?" She shook her head. "And when I tried to get information out of her on what happened, she just said that the whole thing was a terrible mistake and refused to say anything more about it. When I try to probe further, she gets irritated with me."

Violet frowned and reached for her friend's hand again. "I'm so sorry. I know how much you were looking forward to this wedding."

"Well, it wasn't for me. I mean I'd feel better if I knew she was happy—and I'm not sure that she is."

"I can understand that." Violet nodded sympathetically.

They lapsed into silence before Violet asked, "So is she seeing someone new or something?"

"That's what I asked her and you'll never guess what she told me."

"What?"

"That she's not interested in dating anyone serious right now. She wants to—" Adele made quotation marks with her fingers "—keep her options open."

Violet's features crumbled into a mask of disbelief. "Wow. That sounds more like something Miles would have said."

Adele tossed her hands up in surrender. "I don't know what's come over her. I leave for two weeks and my daughter has turned into someone I don't recognize. And now, she's on this health kick. Yesterday when we went out for lunch, she told me every horrible disease I could die from with each item listed on the menu."

"My friend Lila is like that. Absolutely drives me crazy when she does things like that. Now I've made it a point whenever I meet her for lunch to order the fattest cheese-burger on the menu—drives her berserk."

"I'll keep that in mind," Adele promised, and then took a sip of her wine. "In the meantime, I guess I'll just have to sit and pray that whatever Destiny is going through is just a phase."

"Hmm," Violet said with a shake of her head.

"What?" Adele asked.

Violet started to say something, and apparently thought better of it as she waved her friend off. "It's nothing."

Adele frowned. "It sure didn't look like nothing."

"Well, I was thinking it would be nice if Miles and Destiny would get together. But it seems as if they are at two different crossroads. I mean, this is the first time Miles has ever considered settling down, but it sounds like it's the last thing on Destiny's mind."

Adele's shoulders slumped forward. "You're right. Judging by the way she was talking yesterday, I'd say she's serious about 'letting her hair down and going whichever way the wind blows.' Besides, you're forgetting one thing—our children can't stand each other."

"Fine. If you're going to nitpick my plan to death, I'll just keep it to myself."

Adele laughed and Violet quickly joined in.

It had come as a great shock for them to discover a few years ago, that the loud, obnoxious man Destiny had often complained about was, in fact, Violet's beloved son. And the stuck-up prude who had pepper-sprayed Miles was none other than Destiny.

Their waiter reappeared and the women were embarrassed that they hadn't selected anything from the menu because they had been running their mouths. So they stuck to their tried and true choices of soup and salad.

"I don't know," Violet said after the waiter left their table.

"I don't remember the whole dating scene being this complicated back when I met Richard."

"I know what you mean," Adele agreed. "I swear the younger generation makes things harder than necessary."

"Amen. Not only that—when you married someone, you were in it for the long haul. None of these two-year marriages."

"You know what I think the problem is? People are exposed to too much and have way too many options."

Violet laughed at her friend.

"I'm being serious. There are actually couples where one partner lives off in New York and the other one lives in Japan somewhere. Relationships surviving off emails and fax machines. I mean, really."

"Where do you get this stuff?"

"I saw it on *20/20* or one of those other news magazine shows. I'm telling you, relationships have definitely changed over the years."

Still laughing, Violet nodded. "Okay, I'll give you that much. Relationships have changed. But there are still those rare people who marry for the long-term and they're happy— despite their many options. I just hope Miles is one of them."

"Yeah. I pray Destiny will find and settle down with a love like I had with her father." She looked over at Violet and shook her head. "It's just too bad our children don't get along."

"Yeah. It's too bad."

On Saturday afternoon, Destiny and Lu Jin met at their favorite hair salon, Motions. Around the stylists' chairs, women eagerly indulged in the latest gossip. At the hairdryers, women exchanged bored looks while reading the magazines from the previous two years; and at the shampoo bowls, Destiny and Lu Jin were enjoying wonderful scalp massages.

"Sean, I swear you have the best hands this side of Georgia." Lu Jin gave him her usual compliment.

"Girl, that's exactly what my man told me the other night," he sassed and favored her with a wink.

Destiny and the new girl that was shampooing her hair laughed.

Sean looked over at them. "That's all right. You can laugh if you want to, but it will never be said that Sean doesn't know how to keep his men happy." He snapped his fingers in the air and swiveled his neck with much attitude. "Okay."

"I hear you, girl," Lu Jin said without missing a beat.

"Men?" Destiny asked amused. "Just how many do you have?"

"Enough to keep me satisfied," Sean answered.

There was a chorus of laughter, which told Destiny that others were tuned into their conversation. "Of course, I hear that you let that fine brother you were dating go. Mind if I call him up?"

Destiny rolled her head toward Lu Jin but thought better of reprimanding her friend in public. However, she made a mental note to herself to give Lu Jin a piece of her mind as soon as they left. "Sure, he's all yours if you think he's your type."

"Tall, dark and rich is always my type," Sean replied and won another chorus of laughter from their audience and even a smile from Destiny.

A few minutes later, Sean and the new girl left Destiny and Lu Jin at the sink with an application of deep conditioner in their hair.

"I'm sorry. I know I shouldn't have told him about you and Jefferson," Lu Jin launched into an apology.

Destiny rolled her eyes and leaned toward her. "You know how much I hate having people in my business—especially in this place."

"I know. I'm sorry. I wasn't thinking." Lu Jin gave her a small pout. "Am I forgiven?"

Destiny pretended to be angry for about half a second and then waved her friend's concern off. "Of course you are. Just don't let it happen again."

"Deal."

"Good." She smiled, and then changed the subject. "You know. I've been doing some thinking."

"That's dangerous—especially here lately."

"Ha-ha. Seriously, what do you think about me opening a law practice?"

"I thought you were giving up law?"

"I was, but after talking with Miles, I've changed my mind."

"Miles helped you change your mind?"

"Well, sort of. He helped me realize that law is as much a part of me as it was Adam. But I need to come up with my own ideas and approach to my career."

"Didn't I tell you that last year?"

"You did?"

This time Lu Jin rolled her eyes. "I guess next you'll start bringing him to Motions instead of me, seeing how you two are becoming such good friends."

"What are you talking about?" Destiny frowned at her.

"I'm talking about all I hear lately is Miles said this or Miles said that. I'm starting to feel as though I've been replaced by your new best friend."

"Don't be ridiculous."

Lu Jin swallowed her retort and rolled her eyes.

"Come on." Destiny leaned over and touched her arm. "We go way back. No one will ever be able to take your place in my heart. No one."

Lu Jin frowned. "I'm sorry," she finally said, looking contrite. "I'm being silly."

Destiny smiled. "It's kind of flattering that you would get jealous, though."

"Don't let it go to your head. I must be PMSing."

"Yeah. That must be it."

They shared a smile.

"So going back to the subject at hand, what do you think of my starting a law practice?"

Lu Jin drew in a deep breath. "Honestly?"

"Preferably."

"I think…it's a great idea."

Destiny's smile brightened; a bubble of giddy anxiety burst within her. "I do, too."

Miles was going to be late. He was supposed to meet Wes and Theo for their final tux fitting for a friend's wedding. That was the problem with the summer. Everyone wanted to get married in the summertime. Rushing out of his apartment, he was surprised to see Jefferson Altman knocking on Destiny's door.

"She's not home," Miles blurted as he locked his door. When he looked back over at Jefferson, he was momentarily shocked to see the crestfallen expression on the man's face. "I believe she went to the hair salon with Lu Jin this morning," he went on to explain.

"Oh." Jefferson looked down at his watch. In his hands he carried another bundle of flowers.

"After that, I believe she said something about meeting her mother somewhere for dinner."

Jefferson exhaled and nodded, but still looked reluctant to leave.

Shrugging, Miles decided to go on his merry way when Jefferson's voice, thick and raw with emotion, halted him.

"You wouldn't happen to know how she's doing, would you?" Jefferson asked.

Miles didn't quite know how to answer the question and he definitely didn't want to be brought into the middle of anything, either. "She seems to be doing all right," he said, hoping to sound as neutral as possible.

"Hmm. I wish I could say the same for me."

Jefferson's admission took Miles by surprise. For one strange moment in time, it seemed as though Jefferson had forgotten their decade-long hatred for one another. And in that same moment, Miles almost felt sorry for the poor fellow— almost.

"If you'd like I can tell her you stopped by."

Jefferson nodded, and then slowly his eyes narrowed suspiciously. "Destiny always gave me the impression that you two weren't close."

The corners of Miles's mouth tilted upward. "We weren't."

Judging by Jefferson's sudden hardened expression, Miles suspected that he'd said the wrong thing.

"What happened to change that?"

Miles held his hands up and shook his head. "I think this is where I say good day." Once again, he turned toward the elevators.

With lightning speed, Jefferson rushed around and blocked his path and threw the flowers at Miles's feet. "Has something happened between you and Destiny?"

Miles paused, giving him time to rein in his sudden flare of irritation. "No," he said simply.

"I don't believe you," Jefferson said through clenched teeth.

Amused, Miles quirked his brow. "I can see that, but it's the truth. Now if you don't mind, I'm running late for an engagement. If you want, you're more than welcome to pick up the mess you just made and sulk at Destiny's door until she returns. I, on the other hand, have better things to do." Miles stepped around him and continued on to the elevator bay.

"She's a wonderful woman," Jefferson called after him.

Miles reacted more to the raw emotion echoing in Altman's voice than what he said. He stepped into the elevator without a backward glance, but once the doors slid closed, he said, "I know."

Chapter 16

Months rolled by while Destiny and Miles became increasingly closer friends. Their daily, early-morning runs moved from two miles up to Miles's customary four. And now they visited the gym two days a week. They spent so much time together there were rumbles of complaints from their other friends.

"Hey, the Super Bowl is next week. Why don't we throw a party?" Destiny suggested, stepping out of the elevator and onto the fourteenth floor.

Miles's brows rose as he considered the suggestion. "You know, that might not be such a bad idea. The guys and I usually watch the game down at the ESPN Zone, but I'm sure they'd love the idea of a party—especially Wes."

"Great. I'll finally get to meet your infamous best friend."

"You've never met Wes?"

"Not officially. I've seen you two together from time to time, but I've never met him."

"Then be prepared for a treat," Miles warned.

"If he's anything like you, then consider it done."

They laughed and turned toward their respective apartments.

"Oh," Destiny said suddenly as a thought occurred to her. "How did your blind date go the other night?"

Miles's head rocked back with a bark of laughter. "You mean the one my mother set me up on?"

"That's the one." A wide grin stretched across Destiny's face in anticipation of a humorous story.

He shook his head and leaned against his door frame. "Longest night of my life. I believe her name was Monica—a five-time divorcée who has never worked a day in her life."

Destiny laughed. "You've got to be kidding?"

"Nope. She's been married to two plastic surgeons, a real estate tycoon, a movie director and a lottery winner—all by the age of thirty."

"Jeez, I feel like such a late bloomer. Maybe I should rethink all this independence stuff."

Miles's laugh deepened. "You would never have trouble finding a rich man to take care of you. You definitely have the looks."

She pressed a hand to her chest. "Why, I believe you just paid me a compliment."

"Sorry." He held up his hands. "It won't happen again."

She smiled. "I can't believe your mother set you up with someone like that."

"Are you kidding? I'm beginning to suspect my mother just wants me married. She couldn't care less to whom."

"I find that hard to believe."

Miles shrugged. "Yeah, maybe I'm pouring it on a bit thick. Chances are my mother didn't really know the girl. She could have been a friend of friend of a friend."

"She has a whole network devoted to getting you hitched?"

"Seems that way."

"Are you regretting ever telling her that you're ready to settle down?"

"Nah. This has been the happiest I've seen her in a long time—so it's worth it."

Destiny shrugged and turned to enter her apartment.

"What about you?" Miles's question stopped her before she could disappear behind the door.

"What about me?"

"Didn't you tell me that you had a date this week?"

She rolled her eyes and nodded. "Tonight."

Again his brows rose as one in mild curiosity. "Tonight?"

"Yeah. Believe it or not, Lu Jin fixed me up on this one."

"In that case, are you sure you won't need a chaperone?"

She laughed. "There's no telling." She turned again.

"So, who's the guy?"

Destiny faced him again and shrugged. "Someone in Lu Jin's theater troupe."

"An actor?" he asked incredulously. "You're actually going out with an actor?"

"What's wrong with going out with an actor?" She frowned, crossed her arms and waited for an answer.

"Surely, you've heard about artsy people—they're strange, emotionally unbalanced and, more often than not, broke."

Destiny's hand covered her mouth, but it did little to stop her burst of laughter. "You've got to be kidding me."

"What? It's true."

She rolled her eyes again. "That has to be the most ridiculous thing I've ever heard."

"Fine." He shrugged. "Go out with him. You'll see."

"All right, I better get going. I'm meeting that real estate agent about some office space up in Buckhead."

He smiled. "So you're really going to go through with this? You're going to start your own business?"

She nodded and drew in a deep breath. "I admit I'm a bit nervous about the whole thing."

"You'll do fine." He waved off her concerns. "This stuff is in your blood."

"That may be so, but after reviewing how much all this is going to cost, I'll be looking for a partner soon." Her smile dropped as her eyes widened. "What about you?"

Miles's smile faltered. "What about me?"

"Why don't *we* become partners?"

"What?" He shook his head. "Oh, no."

"Why not you? You're a decent lawyer."

"Gee, thanks."

"And you have capital."

"How come I feel like I'm back out on my date with Monica?"

"Come on. I'm being serious." She crossed the hall to his apartment just as he turned and entered it, trying to get away from her.

"My answer is no," he said, moving farther away from her.

She followed. "Miles, this whole thing was *your* idea."

"It was my idea that *you* start your own practice—not me. I have no interest in leaving my lofty position at Mortensen and Foster so I can throw my money away."

"What's the big deal? You're expecting to die in a few years anyway. This way you can just will me a small fortune to keep the practice running."

Flabbergasted, he jerked toward her. "Ouch. You really know how to hurt a fella."

She gave him an apologetic smile, but pushed further. "I want you to be my partner."

"You mean you want my money."

"Okay, fine." She shrugged. "I want your money."

Miles plopped down on his sofa. "Now how can I say no to an offer like that?"

She perked up. "Really? You'll do it?"

"No," he said solemnly. "Learn to recognize sarcasm."

Undaunted, she joined him on the sofa. "Come with me to look at the office space. You'll love it and we're getting a great deal."

Miles only laughed as she went on to describe the locale of their potential business. "I am not listening to you, Destiny."

"What do you think of Brockman and Stafford, Attorneys at Law?" She spread her hands out as if picturing it on a marquee.

"Why is your name first?"

"Okay, then, Stafford and Brockman, Attorneys at Law. You sure do know how to drive a hard bargain."

"Stop it." He jumped back onto his feet. "I'm not going to do it."

"Give me one good reason why not."

"I make pretty good money where I am. I have no desire to lose any."

Destiny rolled her eyes. "Oh, come on. Live a little—while you have the time."

He waved a finger at her. "You're making fun of a dying man."

"All right. I take it back. I should have known you didn't have the guts to try and do something like this anyway." She shook her head and turned to leave. "Besides, you're not that good of a lawyer anyway."

"What?" he thundered, following her to the door. "I'm a damn good lawyer."

"Oh, right. I forgot. You're just too chicken to take a risk."

"You're actually going to bait me by calling me chicken?" She clucked.

"You're being ridiculous."

She clucked louder.

"I'm not afraid to take a risk."

Louder.

"All right, already. I'll go see the building."

With a squeal of delight, Destiny jumped, threw her arms around him and kissed him soundly on the lips. And just as quickly, the world tilted on its axis, spinning Destiny into a vortex of something strange and wondrous. Her thoughts muddled as she suddenly felt as light as air while suspended in his arms.

Unsure of why or even where she found the strength, Destiny drew back and ended their kiss. She sucked in huge gulps of air and her breasts heaved teasingly against his broad chest, making it that much harder to clear her head.

"I think you can put me down now," she finally managed to say.

Miles blinked and a cloud of confusion lifted from his eyes. "Sorry," he said, and then coughed to clear his throat. After he set her down, his usual jovial mood returned. "Hell, had I known that's what it took to get a kiss like that from you, I would have offered you money a long time ago."

She punched his arm. "Just consider it a one-time sign-on bonus," she sassed. "Now hurry up and get dressed, I'm suppose to meet the real estate agent in an hour. It shouldn't take us long to look over everything and then I can make it back here in time for my date."

"Yes, Your Highness."

He was rewarded another punch.

"Ouch." He frowned and rubbed his shoulder. "All right, all right. I'll jump in the shower and meet you in a few. That is unless you want to join me in the shower." He jiggled his brows at her.

"I'll pass." She shook her head and rolled her eyes before turning to leave. "See you in a few, partner," she said over her shoulder.

* * *

Exactly an hour later, Destiny and Miles pulled up in front of the vacant office space in the heart of Buckhead.

Miles got out of the car emitting a low whistle before glancing over at Destiny. "When you dream, you dream big, don't you?"

A wide smile monopolized her face as she slammed her car door. "Why not?"

He shook his head and glanced back up at the building.

"So what do you think?" she finally asked after a lengthy silence had passed.

Drawing in a deep breath, Miles rocked back on his heels and looked over at her. "Do you have any idea how much an endeavor like this is going to cost us?"

She nodded and her smile grew even wider.

Miles's eyes narrowed suspiciously. "What's so funny?"

She walked around the car to loop an arm through his. "You said 'us.'"

Despite everything, he smiled, too. "I did, didn't I?" He shook his head, convinced he was losing his marbles for even considering this. It was a risk—a big one. But hadn't he always liked taking risks? He looked at her again. He knew firsthand that she was one hell of a lawyer and would be a wise choice for anyone to consider partnering.

He took a moment and listened to both the angel and the devil advocates that sat on his shoulders while they deliberated the issue between themselves before reaching an impulsive decision.

Destiny launched into his arms. "I swear you won't regret this."

"Sure I will." He shook his head, and then smiled down at her. "Partner."

But in the end…

Chapter 17

Five years later

"Surprise!"

Miles's mouth dropped at the sight of a hundred plus people gathered in The Waverly Hotel's grand ballroom. He blinked and turned toward an elated Wes.

"You didn't think we forgot about you, did you, buddy?" Wes beamed and pounded him proudly on the back.

The crowd burst into a chorus of "Happy Birthday."

Destiny stepped forward, wearing a stunning spaghetti-strapped red dress. It was transparent in the midriff and showed off her spectacular abs. Her hair, or lack of, was a low crop of curls that gave attention to her long neck and elegant bone structure. As she moved closer, Miles's gaze fell to the deep split on her dress's right side and paid closer attention to her shapely legs.

When she reached his side and rocked onto her toes, he leaned down and received a kiss on the cheek.

"Happy forty-fifth," she murmured against his ear.

"I can't believe you guys did all of this," he said.

"Nothing's too good for my favorite partner." She winked at him.

The song ended and the room exploded into applause as everyone chanted, "Speech, speech, speech."

Tongue-tied and embarrassed, Miles was reluctant to give in to their demands. In the next instant, a drink was shoved into his hand, and both Wes and Destiny encouraged him to give the crowd what they wanted.

He held up his hand while his mind scrambled for something to say. The noise died down as he cleared his throat. "What can I say? You guys really got me on this one." Miles flashed everyone a brief, but genuine, smile.

Laughter rippled through the crowd.

"Well, you all know me. I've never been one for making speeches, but I will say that I'm very flattered by all the trouble you must have gone thought to pull this off, especially for my good friend Wes here." He looped an arm around his friend's neck and pulled him closer. "This is the first time I've ever known him to keep a secret."

The crowd laughed.

"Ouch." Wes winced.

Miles removed his arm and then gestured to Destiny. "So for now, I'll assume that my lovely partner in crime had a lot to do with this—and I humbly thank her."

She slid an arm around his waist and then smiled at the crowd. "There's plenty of food and drinks so everybody have a good time."

Everyone applauded, while Miles, Destiny and Wes moved into the crowd.

"I can't believe you guys," Miles said with a smile still hugging his lips.

"Well, if this does turn out to be your last birthday, we wanted you to go out with a bang," Wes replied with a hearty laugh.

"Wes!" Destiny reprimanded and stomped her foot.

Lu Jin suddenly appeared from behind Wes and popped him on the back of the head. "I swear you have the sensitivity of a gnat," she chastised.

"What?" Wes held a hand to the back of his head. "He knows I was just joking."

Miles laughed. "It's okay. Wes is just being Wes. But I can tell you one thing. I can easily get used to you girls being my personal defense attorneys."

"I just bet you could," Destiny said, shaking her head.

Lu Jin moved closer to Miles and kissed him on the cheek. "Happy Birthday."

"Thank you."

"Is there any room for me?"

Miles's smile grew brighter at the sight of his mother. He opened his arms to receive her and the tender kiss she gave him. "Happy birthday, dear," she said.

"I'm so glad you're here," he said, hugging her.

"Of course I am. I even managed to drag Brother Vernon here." She winked.

Miles scanned the crowd for his mother's date. When he didn't see him, he gave her a warning look. "You make sure he has you home at a decent hour. I don't trust him with my favorite girl."

Despite herself, she blushed and smacked Miles's chest. "Oh, go on."

He kissed her again. "I mean it—midnight, Cinderella."

She waved off his mock concerns with a dismissive hand and disappeared back into the crowd.

"I hope the birthday boy isn't planning on keeping my date hostage all night."

Miles turned to see a young, but distinguished-looking man standing behind him.

Destiny slipped from Miles's light embrace and eased next to the stranger. "Of course not," she assured the man.

Miles cleared his throat.

"Oh, where are my manners?" Destiny asked, shaking her head. "Steve, I want you to meet my law partner, Miles Stafford. Miles, this is Steven Bennett. He's a good friend of mine."

Wes masked the word 'bull' with a loud cough and caused Miles to smile.

Destiny shot Wes a stern look, while Lu Jin rewarded him with another whack on the head.

To Steve's credit, he kept a good-natured smile on his face as he accepted Miles's extended hand.

"It's nice to meet you," Miles said. "I would say that Destiny has told me all about you, but..." He shrugged.

"That's because we just met last month at Justin's," Steve offered as an explanation.

Miles looked at her and winked. "Is that right—last month?"

In response, Destiny looped an arm around Steve's waist. "I think it's time we mingled."

"Yeah, you do that," Miles said.

"It was nice meeting you," Steve said as Destiny pulled him away.

"Same here." Miles nodded and watched as the couple disappeared into the crowd. Then he turned back to Wes and Lu Jin. "How old is that guy?"

Wes shrugged. "I don't know, but I'm sure if we searched his tricycle we could find a set of Mouseketeer ears."

Lu Jin crossed her arms. "You two need to stop playa-hating."

"What?"

She shook her head. "No one ever says anything when men date younger women so why should it be any different for a woman?"

"Oh, here we go again." Wes rolled his eyes. "This is hardly the place to start a bra-burning ceremony."

"What's that supposed to mean?" Lu Jin demanded, jabbing her hands on her hips.

Miles snickered at the brewing fight.

Wes tried to drape an arm around Lu Jin, but she side-stepped his efforts. "Don't touch me."

"If you two would excuse me, I think I'm going to go and get something from the bar," Miles said, but doubted that the combustible friends heard him.

As he moved through the crowd, people continued to send him good wishes and congratulate him for reaching his most dreaded forty-fifth birthday. He doubted that anyone suspected the ball of anxiety anchored in the center of his stomach.

Out of the corner of his eyes, he caught a glimpse of Destiny's red dress. His gaze focused on her and her young companion, and he found he couldn't take his eyes off of them.

In the past five years, Destiny's commitment to diet and exercise had paid off and she had built one incredible body. She also moved and radiated a confidence that was unmatched. As he stared at her, it wasn't the first time he wondered if his brotherly affection toward her wasn't turning into something deeper.

He shook his head. "Don't be ridiculous," he said under his breath, but his eyes kept flickering in her direction. Even in a crowded room where a live band was performing, he was able to zero in on her melodious laughter from across the room.

"You're staring again," Wes said suddenly from behind him.

Miles drew in a deep breath and pulled his large frame erect. "I was not staring."

"Uh-huh." Wes sounded unconvinced and looked in Destiny's direction. "Then you'd be the only man in the room who wasn't. It should be against the law for a woman to look that good."

Miles exhaled, but even to his ears it sounded more like a sigh. "You know the deal between me and Destiny. We're just friends."

Wes's gaze shot to his friend just before rolling heavenward. "You sound more like a parakeet every day." He shook his head again. "We're just friends. We're just friends," he mimicked. "The only one swallowing that B.S. is you. And I'm not too sure if you're buying it, either."

Miles opened his mouth to respond, but his words were cut off by a syrupy sweet, feminine voice calling his name. He turned as a slender arm slid around him.

"Celeste," he greeted with a warm smile. "What are you doing here?"

"I hope you don't mind. When Wes told me about this little party, I just couldn't resist." She leaned up and kissed him. "So how have you been?"

Destiny found Steve's sarcastic humor a riot. Laughing at another one of his wild witticisms, she caught sight of Miles from across the room with a familiar face. Steve's words faded into the background as her mind scrambled for where she'd seen the attractive woman next to Miles before.

When she couldn't remember, she experienced a strong urge to go and investigate.

Don't be ridiculous. She turned her attention back to Steve and realized that she had no idea what he was rambling about. When he paused, she took it as her cue to laugh and hoped that it was the appropriate response.

Steve smiled and she was relieved that her attention lapse went undetected. But she was still itching to work her way back over to Miles to solve the puzzle of the mysterious woman. Then, she had an idea. She tilted up her glass and in one long gulp, drained the champagne.

Steve's brows crowded together as he stared at her.

Destiny came up for air and held her empty glass toward him. "Could I trouble you for a refill?"

Slowly, he reached for her glass and said, "Sure."

No sooner had he turned his back, Destiny pivoted and made a beeline toward Miles.

"We should try and get together some time."

Destiny caught the tail end of what the woman was saying.

"That sounds good to me," Miles said.

Destiny frowned, then immediately put on her best smile as she interrupted the cozy couple. "So how's everything going?" She stepped between them. "Is everyone having a good time?"

Miles smiled and moved to stand by his girl friend. "Everything's great. Destiny, you remember Celeste Silverman?"

The pretty woman offered her hand. "It's been a long time."

Destiny accepted the hand, clueless to the woman's identity.

"You have no idea who I am, do you?" Celeste asked.

Destiny started to deny it, but then figured it was best to be honest. "I'm sorry. But you do look familiar."

"Actually, I was there when you two met for the first time. You were just moving into the apartment across from Miles ten years ago."

"Oh, yes," Destiny said with the memory resurfacing. "How have you been?" She casually checked the woman's hand for a wedding ring and was disturbed to find her fingers bare.

"Great. I hope you don't mind me crashing your party, but I sort of heard about it through the grapevine—or rather Wes."

"Of course not. I'm glad you could come," Destiny lied with relative ease.

"You know a few years ago when I heard you two went into business together, I couldn't believe it."

"There you are." Steve moved in to join the small group. "I was wondering where you'd sneaked off to." He handed Destiny her drink.

"Thank you." She smiled.

The band struck up an instrumental of *Beautiful Ones* and Celeste turned toward Miles. "I know this is out of character, but would you like to dance?"

"I'd love to," he responded, smiling. He looked back to Destiny and Steve. "Would you excuse us?"

"Certainly," Steve answered.

Destiny said nothing. She simply watched the retreating couple with a feigned smile.

"Well, he seems like a nice guy," Steve commented, easing an arm around Destiny.

She didn't hear him.

"He also seems to have a great deal of interest in you."

"Huh? What?" She turned toward him.

"And if I didn't know any better I'd say you're more than a little interested in him, as well."

"Oh, don't be silly. Miles and I are just good friends."

"I've never known friends to look at each other the way you do." Though his words were accusatory, his voice held a note of patient sincerity.

Shaking her head, she eased closer to him, purposely brushing her body against his in a suggestive manner. "I don't detect a hint of jealousy, do I?"

He quirked a brow at her as a mischievous smile curved his lips. "Should I be jealous?"

She leaned forward and kissed him. "Not at all," she murmured when she pulled away. "Not at all."

* * *

Miles frowned at the sight of Destiny and Steve's open affection. He rolled his eyes. "If they are going to behave like that, I wish they'd just get a room," he grumbled.

Celeste followed his gaze, and looked suspiciously at him. "Is there something going on between you guys?"

When he didn't respond, she tapped him on the shoulder. "Miles?"

"Huh?" He looked back at Celeste and had the sinking feeling that he'd just been caught not paying attention. "Oh, I was just…" He paused not really knowing how to finish the sentence.

She drew in a deep breath. "Yeah. I know what you were doing."

"I'm sorry. That was rude of me."

She studied him.

"What?" he asked finally.

"I'm trying to judge whether you're the same old Miles Stafford I knew ten years ago—the consummate bachelor."

His smile waned. It was his turn to study her. "I hurt you once, didn't I?"

Her answer was quick and honest. "Deeply."

"I'm sorry," he responded in equal measure. "Forgiven?"

"Yes." Celeste smiled. "It was a long time ago."

"Friends?"

"Friends."

Miles nodded, and then pulled her close and began to sway in time to the music. In the distance, he heard Destiny's laughter and like a moth to a flame his gaze sought her in the crowd.

Chapter 18

Lu Jin gestured toward the dance floor. "Will you just look at them?"

Wes shook his head and gulped down his drink. "I know. It's sickening, isn't it? I wish they'd just jump each other's bones and get it over with."

"Who do Miles and Destiny think they're fooling? One looking at the other when they're not looking and vice versa." She turned away from the dance floor, shaking her head. "They need counseling."

"More like they need a bed."

"Amen," Theo and Juan said, joining them at the bar.

"Who has the bet for this month as being the month they finally sleep together?" Juan asked.

Elliott held up a hand. "That would be me and judging by what's going on on the dance floor, you can all just fork over my money now."

Lu Jin shook her head. "Nah, not tonight. Or did you miss that Destiny brought a date?"

Elliott laughed. "He has to go home sometime. Or did you forget that Destiny and Miles still live next door to each other?"

"I heard *that!*" Wes held up his hand and the two men gave each other high fives.

"I still say you're wrong," she said stubbornly.

"Uh-huh. You're just mad because your bet is for December. Hell, you may be planning a baby shower by that time."

The men laughed.

"You all can just go to hell. Besides, that's what you've said for the last two years."

"You know there's a chance they've already slept together and haven't told us," Theo suggested.

Wes and Lu Jin looked at each other and considered the possibility then shook their heads. "Nah," they said in unison.

Across the room, Adele watched the coy glances darting between Destiny and Miles with a knowing smile.

Violet leaned over and whispered into her friend's ear. "The way I figure it, we'll be in our nineties by the time they figure things out."

Adele laughed. "Surely not that long."

"I don't know. Miles may have graduated at the top of his class, but I'm beginning to suspect that he's not the sharpest tool in the toolbox when it comes to romance."

"I can testify the same for Destiny," Adele said with pursed lips.

"Any ideas on how we can get them together?"

"Not a clue—you?"

Violet exhaled a long tired breath. "None. I've been shoving the idea of him dating Destiny down his throat every chance I get, but all he does is laugh and say—"

"We're just good friends," Adele finished the sentence since she'd been getting the same response from Destiny.

"Maybe we should just face the fact that we're lousy at playing Cupid and leave them to their own destruction."

The women looked at each other, and then wicked smiles bloomed across their faces as they responded in unison, "Nah."

Miles tapped Steve on the shoulder and interrupted his slow dance with Destiny. "Mind if the birthday boy cuts in?" he asked with an amicable smile.

Steve looked as if he wanted to refuse the request, but he glanced back at Destiny then said, "Of course not." He stepped away.

Miles thanked him and pulled Destiny into his arms. "I didn't think I had a chance of prying you two apart, judging by the way you're all over each other."

Destiny laughed and swayed in time to the music. "Are you playing the part of the overprotective brother again?"

He shrugged. "Since the job is available, I don't see the harm. Do you?"

"I don't think Steve sees it that way," she said honestly. "He already thinks there's something going on between us. After this dance, I'm going to have a hard time convincing him otherwise."

"Uh-huh. Since when did you start scanning the scene at Justin's for dates?"

"I met a client there for drinks during Happy Hour." She shrugged casually. "Steve approached me and made me laugh, so I agreed to go out with him."

"You don't think Junior's too young?"

"He's legal so I don't see a problem."

Miles laughed. "I can think of at least a thousand reasons why dating him is a bad idea, Mrs. Robinson."

"Hey, I'm not above teaching the younger generation a few things."

Miles's handsome features hardened into a scowl.

Destiny laughed at his reactions and thought how much he reminded her of Adam whenever they talked of the men she dated in college. He, too, never had a kind word for any of them and constantly thought she was too good for them.

"So what else do you know about our little teenager?"

"For one thing, I know he's *not* a teenager."

"What does he do for a living? Or is he having a hard time getting his parents to sign a work permit for McDonald's?"

She slapped him on the arm. "Behave. I'll have you know he's a financial analyst for Smith and Barney."

"Successful?"

"Very."

"Hmm." He looked over his shoulder and found Steve standing on the edge of the dance floor, watching them. Miles waved and flashed him a smile. "Maybe I shouldn't have interrupted you guys."

Laughing, she turned in Miles's arms and caught Elliott giving her the thumbs-up signal. Not understanding his meaning, she frowned.

Wes pulled his attention away from the dance floor and leaned closer to Lu Jin while they stood near the bar. "So when are you going to give up the ghost and go out with me?"

The smile Lu Jin held seconds before disappeared. "Shortly before the second coming of the Lord," she answered, shaking her head.

"Good. I hear he's coming in the morning so why don't we cut out of here and head on over to my place for one last night of sin? I'll supply the baby oil."

She laughed at his quick comeback. "Two points for Wes."

"How many points do I have to get before I get a chance to hit a home run?"

Cocking her head, she settled a hand on her hip. "You're

a million points away from even being able to step into the batter's box."

Undaunted by her flippant response, Wes blew a kiss in her direction. "You know, there's something that I've been meaning to ask you."

"What?" she asked impatiently.

"You know last year when you played a prostitute in that Denzel Washington flick?"

"Stop. Because I can already tell you're treading on thin ice."

He smirked. "I was just wondering where you did your research."

Lu Jin's eyes narrowed. "I simply riffled through your little black book and interviewed all the women you've dated." She turned on her heels and stalked off.

Wes winced, but then a slow smile crept across his face. "Damn, she's beautiful when she's mad."

Theo chuckled from behind him. "I'm not quite sure I'm following your plan on winning Lu Jin's heart. Every time I see you two together, she looks angry."

"You're mistaken, my friend," Wes said, turning toward him. "Her anger masks an even deeper feeling—passion."

Theo chuckled. "Whatever, man. Whatever."

Miles and Destiny continued dancing into their third song together. With the greatest of ease and familiarity they glided across the floor oblivious to knowing smiles and conspiratorial whispers.

"Thank you," Miles said with a deep sincerity.

She leaned back in his arms and studied him. "For the party?"

"For everything," he answered.

"It was my pleasured. Of course, I had to fight Wes on

inviting strippers and holding a wet T-shirt contest. Other than that, I think the night has turned out to be a great success."

Miles's body quaked with laughter. "He can get a bit carried way when it comes to parties."

"*Now* you tell me."

His eyes still twinkling, he guided her gracefully across the floor. "I don't mind telling you that you're the best-looking lady in the room. New hairstyle?" He referred to her new short crop.

She tilted her chin up, giving him a great view of her elegant bone structure and asked, "You like it?"

"Amazingly, I do. I think if you'd asked me before you whacked it all off, I'd probably have thought it a bad idea. But seeing it now, I have to say it definitely suits you."

"So glad you approve."

Miles smiled and continued to stare down at her.

"How are you feeling, really?" she asked, misunderstanding his silence. "Are you okay with turning forty-five?"

His gaze finally deserted her face. "I'll feel better when I turn forty-six."

"You will," she said, inching closer. "Because I have an even bigger party planned for next year."

Her comment solicited yet another laugh from him. "We'll see." He spun her in his arms and enjoyed dancing with her until the end of the song, when Steve finally returned for his date.

Miles retreated to the arms of Celeste, but there was never a moment when he didn't know exactly where Destiny was or what she was doing.

Chapter 19

Miles absolutely loved the taste of Destiny's mouth, her neck and her breasts. It was all he could do to hold on to what little sanity he had left while her hips rocked against him.

The room spun while the only air he could get into his lungs came in short ragged spurts. Her dewy walls sheathed and massaged him into dizzying heights—so much so he swore he'd never come down.

The sound of his name tumbling from her lips also had a heady affect. He plunged deeper. He loved her cries of euphoria and loved the sight of her flushed burgundy face.

A rush of heat whirled within, he could feel his body building to a sweet release when—

Miles's alarm clock blared from the nightstand and his arm shot out from beneath the sheets to bang the snooze button. He slammed his eyes closed and tried to return to his dream, but he couldn't. He groaned with disappointment and sat up in bed. The dreams he had of Destiny were sweet, but he knew that was all they would ever be—dreams.

On the morning after his forty-fifth birthday, he climbed out of bed in time to watch the sunrise. It had turned out to be a growing habit of his in recent years, and he found that the peaceful scenery did wonders to calm his soul.

He drew in a deep cleansing breath and reflected over last night's events. It was just like Destiny to try and make his birthday a special event. Every year, she went out of her way to find some obscure jazz record or rare comic book she knew he wanted.

Smiling, he couldn't imagine what life would ever be like without Destiny's friendship.

And then his thoughts turned dark. The results from his last physical reported that he was in perfect health, but he knew the inevitable would still happen and he wondered how his death would occur. Would he be at the wrong place at the wrong time, catch a stray bullet or, better yet, would the brakes on his car mysteriously give out?

Shaking his head, Miles moved away from the window. If he was still going to meet Destiny for their morning run, he'd better get a move on.

As he dressed, he made a promise to himself not to discuss his gloomy thoughts and prayed that Destiny wouldn't bring it up. He'd never been a fan of pity parties and the last thing he wanted to do was have one in his honor.

"It's about time you finally got your lazy butt up." Wes smirked from the kitchen.

Miles's head jerked in his direction. "What are you doing here?"

"Raiding your refrigerator. What does it look like?" He shook his head as he scanned the contents. "Do you ever eat anything other than health food? Haven't you heard that too much of a good thing is also bad for you?"

"I'll keep that in mind. Now do you want to tell me what you're doing here?"

"Maybe I just came by to make sure that you did, in fact, wake up this morning." He shrugged.

Miles smirked. "Am I to believe that you were actually worried about me?"

Pulling out a carton of eggs, Wes rolled his eyes. "Just don't let it go to your head. Besides, I told you this family curse thing was a bunch of bull. You look fine to me."

"I've never said that we died exactly on our forty-fifth birthday, only that we never make it to forty-six."

Wes shook his head. "Whatever. How about I make the birthday boy an omelet?"

"I'll have to eat it when I get back." He looked at his watch. "You know Destiny and I take our morning run together."

"Jeez, I can't believe you haven't nailed her, yet."

"How many times do I have to tell you that it isn't like that between us? She's like a sister to me."

"Uh-huh. Well, I got a sister and I don't go jogging with her every morning. I don't work with her every day or hang out with her after work, and I certainly don't live across the hall from her. For two supposedly smart people, you guys have to be the dumbest I've ever met—and that's saying something."

Miles simply smiled. "If you don't understand by now, then nothing I say is going to make a difference."

Wes rustled a pan from a lower cabinet. "Don't get me wrong. I like Destiny. She's nice, beautiful and has beautiful friends."

Miles laughed at his reference to Lu Jin—who had always treated Wes like something stuck on the bottom of her shoe.

"But—" Wes held up a finger "—I think you need to be honest with yourself."

Miles crossed his arms. "Meaning?"

"Meaning—the reason that you've come up empty on your so-called search for Mrs. Miles Stafford is because you're looking for someone just like your next-door neighbor."

"That's not true."

Wes raised an inquisitive brow. "It's not? You mean you're not looking for a woman you want to spend every waking minute with?"

"That's not what I said."

"And while I'm on a roll here—what woman you know is going to be cool with all the time you do spend with Destiny?"

Miles paused.

"Uh-huh. No woman either of us have ever met." Wes cracked an egg into the skillet. "You should think about it."

Miles headed toward the door. "You sound just like my mother. There's nothing to think about. Destiny and I are friends and that's just the way we like it."

"What's the big deal?" Wes called out to him.

Miles turned toward his friend again.

"Really? What's the worst thing that could happen if you two did decide to date?"

Miles didn't answer. Instead, he turned and exited the apartment. He waited a few minutes in the hall before Destiny's door cracked open, but instead of Destiny rushing out to meet him, he came face-to-face with Steven Bennett.

A flash of anger hardened Miles's features.

Steve's shocked expression suddenly turned mischievous. "Morning."

Miles didn't reply.

Closing the door behind him, Steve crossed his arms. "Quite an arrangement you two have here. You're partners at the office and even live across from each other."

Forcing an air of nonchalance, Miles smiled. "It seems to work for us."

Annoyance flashed in Steve's eyes. "You want to know what I'm wondering?"

"I can't imagine."

"I'm wondering, if you do have a thing for each other, why

neither of you have acted on your feelings. I mean, ten years is a long time—too long if you ask me."

"Next time I'm doing a consensus, Junior, I'll make sure I knock on your door. Besides," he went on to add, "there's nothing going on between Destiny and I."

Steve nodded and uncrossed his arms. "That was my conclusion." He moved away from the door and headed toward the elevators, but not before he added, "Lucky for me."

Seconds later, Destiny rushed out of the apartment. "Sorry I kept you waiting," she exhaled her apology in a flurry of movement.

Miles glared at her. "I can't believe you."

She looked up at him perplexed. "Can't believe what? What did I do?"

"I just said hello to your *boyfriend*. Didn't you say that you just met him?"

"My who? Oh, you mean Steve?"

"Yes, I mean *Steve*. Or do you have more men stashed in your apartment this early in the morning?"

She laughed. "What has gotten into you? Steve is hardly my boyfriend. We just met."

Miles didn't trust himself to speak. The alternative of what she was implying was too troublesome.

"He just stopped by this morning to tell me how much he enjoyed your party last night." She crossed her arms and stared at him. "Or didn't you notice that he wasn't wearing the same clothes he had on last night?"

Blood instantly drained from Miles's face as an awkward silence expanded between them.

She shook her head and locked her apartment door. "And if something had happened between Steve and I, brother dear, it wouldn't be any of your business."

"Can we change the subject since I've made a complete ass out of myself?"

"Gladly," she said, heading toward the elevators. "How are you feeling this morning?"

"Good," he said, wishing she'd chosen another line of questioning. He knew exactly what her next question would be.

"Any anxieties?"

He pressed the down button for the elevator. "None that I can think of," he lied.

She eyed him suspiciously.

He knew she was trying to decide whether she believed him. He suspected she didn't, but she said nothing to support that theory. In fact, she changed the subject.

"Lu Jin and I are going to go check out that house I told you about in Alpharetta."

"So you're really going to leave me?"

Destiny reached up and gently cupped his cheek. "Aw. Are you going to miss me?"

"We've been neighbors for ten years. What do you think?"

"I think you're going to be just fine." She pinched his cheek again. "You're a big boy."

"I'm glad you've noticed." He puffed out his chest and made an arm curl to show his muscles.

"I'm your friend. I'm not blind." She flirted with a wink.

Miles raised a surprised brow. "Feeling a little feisty today, aren't you?"

She shrugged. "What can I say? I'm in a good mood. Besides, we'll still see each other at the office." She flashed him a brief smile. "But it's nice to know that you'll miss me."

As if standing beneath the sun, Miles was warmed by her bright smile. In the past few years, the bond he shared with Destiny had strengthened to the point where he couldn't remember what life had been like before they were friends—or when their friends weren't friends.

It did take Destiny and Lu Jin a while to get used to Wes's wild parties and attention-grabbing antics, but in the end, everyone got along.

"Whatcha thinking about?" Destiny inquired a mile into their run.

"Nothing. I was just going over some details of the Nelson Rogers case," he lied.

Destiny shook her head. "I wish you'd listened to me and rejected that case. The man is a slimeball."

"Slimeballs have rights, too."

"So you keep telling me."

"And they have money. And after losing our ass on that Terri Morris case you wanted so badly, we need all the slimeballs we can find."

She cut her eyes over at him. "You're never going to let me live that one down, are you?"

He smiled at her. "Not if I can help it."

Destiny laughed and picked up her pace, enjoying the slight burn coursing through her calves as she tackled an incline on the park's trail. She remembered a time when such a hill would have done her in.

She glanced back at Miles and noticed another dazed expression had fallen over his features and she wondered if he'd been honest about what was troubling him. She opened her mouth to question him again, but thought better of it. He would tell her when he was ready—like he always did.

"So what do you have on your agenda for today?" she inquired instead.

"Run over to my mother's like I do every Saturday and hang out with Wes this evening."

"What? No date?"

"No. Thank God. I'm about ready to toss in the towel on finding Mrs. Right."

Destiny wasn't fooled, she knew exactly what was troubling Miles—that damn family curse. Of course, her heart dropped a notch at the thought of her being wrong.

"So what about you?" he asked suddenly.

She shrugged. "After I run by the office for a couple hours, I'm going house shopping with Lu Jin and my mother, and then I do have a date."

As usual, his brows shot up when he barked, "With who?"

"What does it matter? You're not going to like him."

"What makes you say that?"

"You've never liked any of the guys I've dated."

"With good reason. And I don't remember being wrong about any of them, either."

She shook her head. "You're impossible—but right."

"So?"

She looked at him puzzled. "So what?"

"So who is it?" he persisted. "And please don't tell me it's that Steve character. There should be a law against—"

"Stop," she said.

"What?"

"You're doing it again."

"Just my opinion," he added flippantly.

Destiny just shook her head, but loved Miles's overprotectiveness. "By the way, you'll never guess what I got in the mail yesterday."

"Can't imagine."

"Come on, guess."

Exasperated, but knowing she wouldn't tell him until he guessed, he took a stab at it. "You won the Publishers Clearing House ten million dollars."

"I wish, but that's not it. I got a wedding invitation—from Jefferson Altman."

"You're joking?" he asked surprised.

"No."

Miles frowned at the fact that his old nemesis obviously

wasn't having the same troubles he had when it came to finding a wife.

"Do you think there's something wrong with me?" Destiny questioned.

"What do you mean?"

She shrugged. "I don't know. He certainly didn't have trouble replacing me and moving on."

"Stop it," he warned.

She looked curiously over at him.

"You're fishing for a compliment again."

"I was not," she answered with a small pout.

"Sure you were. You wanted me to tell you that no one could ever replace you and blah, blah, blah."

She frowned. "Boy, aren't you in a pissy mood."

He laughed. "I just know how that little mind of yours works."

"Humph." She rolled her eyes. "Like it would have hurt you to pay me a compliment."

"So are you going to the wedding?"

"Why—so he can rub it in my face that he's moved on? I don't think so."

They rounded another bend before Miles said, "Maybe there's something wrong with us. We've both been searching for what I'm beginning to think isn't out there."

She frowned as she looked over at him. "Boy, you really are down today."

He shook his head as their high-rise came into view. "I'm just being honest. It just seems nearly impossible to find a quality woman nowadays."

"Whoa." She slowed down to jog in place. "That's not true. There are plenty of quality women. You're just looking in all the wrong places."

"Come on. You know what I'm saying is true. The women I keep running into are more interested in where I live, what

I drive and how much is in my bank account. Sure, they all try to hide it, but sooner or later it all comes out in the open."

"We're not all like that," she insisted. "And while we're on the subject—the guys running around here aren't exactly worth writing home about, either."

"What?"

"You heard me. When I first met you, you were changing women like you changed your clothes. And now that you're ready to settle down, you expect Miss Perfect to show up on your timetable. Well, love doesn't work like that. You reap what you sow." With her temper barely in check, she began jogging again.

Miles quickly caught up with her. "Did I miss something?"

She drew in a deep, steady breath and seemed to calm down.

"Desi?"

She glanced at him and favored him with a quick smile. "No. You didn't miss anything. It's just that I had this same conversation with Elliott and Zack the other day. I know for a fact there are plenty of good women out there, myself included. The problem is we have to put up with all these guys who want to be playas and have their women look like video vamps and have low IQs."

Miles shook his head. "Like you said, we're not all like that. Besides, I know a lot of playas that have changed their ways when the right woman came along. The problem is we have to navigate through those vamps to get to the right person."

"If you know so many good men, then why haven't you ever set me up with one of them?" Destiny asked curiously as they entered their building.

A formidable frown marred his handsome features to the point that he looked like he was scowling. "Set you up?"

She nodded.

"With one of my friends?"

Puzzled, yet entertained by his reaction, Destiny smiled as she crossed her arms and stared at him. "Yeah, why not? Someone other than Wes, of course." When he continued to look disbelievingly at her, she went on. "What's the matter?"

The elevator arrived and they stepped on.

"Well?" she probed. "Or were you just pulling my leg about knowing so many good men?"

Finally, his furrowed brows relaxed. "All right." He pressed the button for the fourteenth floor. "But you have to do the same thing for me."

"Meaning?"

"Meaning, you have to find me a date with one of your quality women, too. And I don't mean Lu Jin. Someone who you truly believe is marriage material."

Destiny's heart skipped a beat at the very thought of having to set him up with one of her friends.

"What?" He smirked. "Can't think of anyone?"

She straightened with fake resolve and rose to the challenge. "You've got yourself a deal."

Chapter 20

When Miles ran the agreement between him and Destiny by Wes, his friend exploded with laughter.

Miles rolled his eyes.

"You want to run that by me again?" Wes cupped his ear toward Miles. "There's got to be something wrong with my hearing."

Miles eased behind his desk as a smile spread across his face. "There's nothing wrong with your hearing."

Wes shook his head. "You're going to find Destiny's Mr. Right and she's agreed to find Mrs. Right for you?"

"That's the arrangement."

Still shaking his head, Wes plopped down in the vacant chair across from Miles. "I swear. You have to be the luckiest bastard alive. Stuff like that never happens to me."

Miles shrugged, but his smile grew wider. "What can I say? Destiny and I just have each other's best interests at heart."

Wes held up his hands in mock surrender. "Please, keep the crap to a bare minimum. I'm not wearing my boots today."

"It makes sense if you think about it," Miles explained. "Who better to set me up than someone who knows me as well as Destiny?"

"What am I—chop suey?" Wes sat upright. "And for the record, this crazy arrangement doesn't make sense to anyone other than you guys. But I'd appreciate it, if you ever do get the urge to jump her bones, if you'd wait until September."

Miles frowned. "September?" Then understanding narrowed his gaze. "Don't tell me that silly bet is still going on."

Wes shrugged; a smile dominated his features. "Hey, September is a great month. The leaves change color, the air is crisp—all that romantic crap women go crazy for."

Miles rocked back into his chair with quakes of laughter. "You need to find something to better occupy your time than a nonexistent romance."

"Are you kidding me? The drama going on between you two is better than what's happening on *Days of Our Lives*."

"Really?" Miles's brows shot up.

Wes cleared his throat. "Not that I've ever watched the show—but I'm guessing."

"Of course you haven't," Miles said, still smiling. "So who has the bid for this month?"

Wes waved his hand absently. "Elliott. He was just convinced you were going to have one hell of a birthday gift to unwrap last night." His twinkling gaze turned suspicious. "You didn't, did you?"

"No," Miles barked, and then added, "not that it's any of your business."

"Yeah, you got to wonder about a girl like that," Wes continued, ignoring Miles's comment. "You got everyone convinced you're going to kick the bucket any minute. You'd think she'd let you hit it—at least out of pity."

"You need to get your head out of the gutter."

"And you need to jump in," Wes countered quickly. "Before you started this wife quest, you were knocking boots like a part-time job. Nowadays, women have to pass a twenty-four-point inspection for you to say hello to them. And now you're telling me that they have to get a stamp of approval from Destiny. As your friend, I'm telling you to lighten up."

With his features scrunched in confusion, Miles asked, "What do you mean?"

"Just what I said." Wes stood from his chair. "It pains me to tell you this, *but you've lost it.* Midas Touch Miles has died, and it's been a messy death to bear witness to, I can tell you that much."

"Come on. It's not that bad."

"Oh, yes it is. You're not the same man I grew up with. You're like a bad, watered-down version of your former self. It's sad. I've made excuses to our friends as to why you're not attending the hot parties. Hell, I've even seen Destiny at a few. And that girl is a freak on the dance floor."

Miles frowned.

"Look, Miles. I know you better than anyone. And whether you want to admit it, you're in love with your next-door neighbor and instead of being a man about the situation, you're staying at home waiting for the realization to dawn on her. How am I doing so far?"

"You're way off base." Miles suspected he would have had better luck convincing Wes had he not hesitated before answering.

Wes's grin took on a wicked quality. "Sure, I am, buddy. Sure I am."

On Monday afternoon, Destiny joined her girlfriends, Debra, Monique and Lu Jin, for lunch. And while everyone chatted nonstop about husbands, boyfriends and children,

Destiny's mind roamed wildly on who would be a good candidate for Miles. The problem was that for every name that scrolled across her brain, she found a major flaw that knocked them off the list.

When Lu Jin leaned over and whispered, "Are you all right?" she nearly jumped out of her skin.

"Oh, yes." She looked guiltily around. "I'm sorry. My mind was roaming."

"That much is apparent." Monique chuckled. "I just want to know if it's that new young thang you're dating that's got your mind up in the clouds."

"Me, too," Debra chimed in with a wicked smile. "The way you two were dancing the other night, I figured you guys got *real* acquainted after the party."

As the women laughed, a wave of embarrassment rippled through Destiny.

Lu Jin elbowed her. "Well?"

Destiny smiled. "You know me, guys—I never kiss and tell."

Everyone moaned in disappointment.

"That's an annoying habit you got there," Lu Jin said, shaking her head. "There should never be secrets between us."

"Are you kidding? Secrets aren't secrets long the way you girls love to gossip."

Their eyes widened as they took in a collective gasp. "Who, us?" they asked in unison.

Destiny laughed. "I love you all, but I'm telling it like it is."

Lu Jin was the first to verbalize her protest. "I'll have you know that we don't gossip. We exchange vital information."

"That's right," Debra and Monique agreed, nodding.

Smiling, Destiny waved them off. "If you say so. I'm not going to argue."

Monique leaned in. "Since you're not going to tell us what

happened when you left the party, surely you're going to tell us how old Steve is."

The women leaned in.

Destiny rolled her eyes. "Steven is twenty-four."

They all squealed with delight.

"Glory be." Lu Jin fanned herself with her hand. "I'm exhausted just thinking about it."

Destiny slapped her hand. "Stop it. You've dated plenty of younger men."

"Never more than three years younger. I don't work out like you. I tire easily."

"I heard that." Monique held up her hand and received excited high fives from the other two women.

Destiny laughed and shook her head. "You girls are out of control."

"*I* want to know what Miles said when he cut in to dance with you," Debra asked. "Now that brotha didn't look too pleased about your date."

Once again, the women leaned forward in rapt attention.

"Ya'll are some nosy women—and you need to get out of my business," Destiny sassed. "But if it's Miles you want to hear about, then maybe you girls can help me with something else."

They bristled at not getting the information they wanted.

"I'm serious. Miles and I were talking the other morning about how hard it is to find quality people to date so we agreed to set each other up. Problem is, I think I just talked myself into a corner because I can't think of anyone that would be perfect for him."

To her surprise, another burst of laughter erupted from her friends. She frowned. "What's so funny?"

They were all so tickled by what she'd said, no one could stop laughing long enough to answer her question.

"What?" Destiny insisted.

Lu Jin pressed a hand against her chest and drew in a deep breath. "Let me get this straight. You're going to find Miles a date?"

Destiny nodded, and then lifted her brows inquisitively when they laughed again. "He's not a bad guy. Any woman should be happy to date him."

"That's not what's so funny," Lu Jin interjected.

"Then what?"

"Come on, Destiny. What have we been telling you for years?"

Rolling her eyes and waving off her friend's comment, Destiny responded more impatiently than she intended. "Don't start that again. I'm being serious."

Eyes still twinkling, Lu Jin met her gaze. "So were we."

Destiny drew in and expelled a tired breath.

Lu Jin went on, "You guys are perfect for each other. I don't see how you can't see it." She counted off her fingers. "You work together, play together—why not sleep together?"

"Three for one," Monique piped in. "You can't beat that."

"Nothing like bargain shopping," Debra added and was the first one to laugh at her clever joke.

All Destiny could manage was a crooked smile.

Lu Jin rolled her eyes. "Oh, come on, Destiny. You mean to tell me that you never once fantasized what it would be like to be with Miles?"

Instantly, she felt trapped by the question.

Her three friends were quick to pick up on her hesitation and they squealed excitedly.

People from surrounding tables turned in their direction and Destiny tried to control her friends.

"Shhh," Destiny said as though she corrected errant children. "We're still in a restaurant, you know."

Apparently unconcerned, Lu Jin continued laughing while managing to say, "You're a fraud, Destiny Brockman."

She rolled her eyes. "Why?"

"Because for the past five years, you've acted like you haven't even noticed he was a member of the opposite sex. Oh, you're smooth."

"Sister girl got game," Monique agreed, and received an impulsive high five from Lu Jin for her commentary.

Destiny shook her head at their antics. "Okay, I know he's a member of the opposite sex—big deal. It doesn't change anything."

Lu Jin waved a finger at her. "It changes everything. And you're crazy if you don't see it. I mean, here is a man you spend practically every waking moment with and you're attracted to him. Honestly, what else can you ask for?"

Debra leaned forward. "If I was you I would be trying to get that man in front of an altar—and soon. Your biological clock is ticking so loud, it's waking me up every morning."

"Not funny," Destiny said with her best silencing glare. "I have plenty of time to have children."

Lu Jin, who had never hid the fact that she didn't consider herself mother material, ticked her finger like a metronome at her. "Do you really want to spend your golden years running to P.T.A. meetings?"

Debra and Monique, who were already mothers, nodded in agreement.

"Don't you think you're being a little dramatic?"

"Am I? Let's say you play the field for another five years. You get married at forty and have children. Your firstborn moves out at eighteen—"

"That's if you're lucky," Debra warned.

"Yeah," Monique nodded.

"You'd be fifty-nine going on sixty. And if you put him through college, tack on another four years."

"He could live on college campus," Destiny argued back.

"Uh-huh, or he could be enrolled at the local community college and live at home."

"Or worse, he could decide that college isn't for him and refuse to move out until he's thirty-five," Monique added gloomily.

The rest of the women looked at her.

"What? It could happen. My brother turned thirty-five last month and he's still home—and has no plans of moving out."

"Okay, stop it, girls. You're starting to depress me. I can appreciate you trying to look out for me and all, but you're wrong about Miles and I." She swallowed and searched for the right words that would finally make them understand. "I know this sounds ludicrous, but in my mind, Miles has sort of filled Adam's shoes."

She stopped and stared at their stunned faces. "He's the big brother I miss having in my life. He loves practicing law. He's overprotective about the men I date. Hell, he even likes the same music as Adam. Now do you understand?"

Their gazes darted from one another, but no one said a word.

"I gotta go," Destiny said, suddenly jumping up from the table.

"Wait, no," Lu Jin protested. "Don't go."

"It's okay." Destiny ignored her, quickly gathering her things. "I've already ruined the mood with my crazy ramblings. I'll catch up with you girls later." She tossed down a twenty onto the table and raced out before her tears won the battle against her willpower.

Chapter 21

Destiny pulled out all of her old newspaper clippings of Adam. The fact that he would stay forever young in her mind and in her heart caused her tears to multiply with each glass of red wine. Taking her time, she reread each word printed in the articles and took each derogatory comment as a personal insult to the memory of the man she knew better than anyone.

For years, she'd tried to put the past just where it belonged—in the past. Yet, the confession to her friends forced her to reexamine her relationship with Miles. Her conclusion: she'd cast Miles in a role he was ill suited to play. She heard a loud ringing, but it took her a moment to realize that it was the phone.

"I'm coming," she mumbled, frowning, and then tried rather awkwardly to get up from the floor. She knocked over the bottle and shrieked in delayed horror as a picture of Adam darkened a deep red.

The phone forgotten, she scrambled back to the floor to

save the other clippings, but made more of a mess than anything else.

"I'm sorry, I'm sorry," she couldn't help repeating as she clutched the damp articles to her body. Before she knew it, she was overcome with emotions that rocked her to her core.

"You have to let me go." Adam's voice, a husky vibrato, was as clear as a bell in her head.

"I'm trying, but it's so hard," she confessed, squeezing her eyes tight.

"Letting go doesn't mean you'll forget me," he said, tenderly.

Destiny stopped rocking, unsure that she'd heard him right.

"It's okay," he assured her again.

At the feathery touch to her shoulder, she opened her eyes to stare into Adam's intense, brown eyes. She pulled back and soaked up his handsome image. He looked as he did the last time she'd seen him alive: the same hair, the same clothes.

Adam smiled and wiped at her tears. Again the touch was light but amazingly cold.

"What's okay?" she asked.

His smile was so tender it broke her heart. "It's okay to let go."

Through fat whelps of tears, Destiny shook her head. "I can't."

He withdrew his hand. "It's been twelve years, Destiny. It pains me that my passing has haunted you like this. It was never my intention to do this to you." He glanced down. "There was a lot that was never my intention."

"You are a part of me. You'll always be a part of me."

"I *was* a part of you. I made mistakes, but they were my mistakes. It hurts my heart to watch you do this to yourself."

She shrugged absently and forced a lie to pass between her lips. "It hasn't been that much of a burden."

Adam smiled. "Don't forget who you're talking to. I know you better than anyone—better than Lu Jin, and better than Miles Stafford. We were twins, after all."

Destiny blinked at his mention of Miles.

"What? You didn't think I knew about him? You did give him some of my best records."

"I—I didn't think you'd mind," she stammered, apologetically.

Adam laughed and she could feel her soul warming to its familiar sound.

"Of course I don't mind," he said, but his smile faded quickly. "But I do mind you throwing your life away. There's no sense in both of us making that mistake."

Destiny frowned. "I haven't thrown my life away. I've built a small, successful law practice." She pulled up from the floor. However, she still felt light-headed and the articles she'd clutched fluttered to the floor.

"And what of your love life?"

She expelled a tired sigh. "Oh, that."

"Yes, that," he said with a note of frustration.

"I'm no super woman. Up until now, my career has occupied most of my time. I mean I date, occasionally—but it's very hard to invest much time in looking for a soul mate." She was rambling, but couldn't help it. "I'm also beginning to suspect all those magazine articles on how a woman can have a successful career and a wonderful family life are just full of crap. It's one or the other if you ask me. Or would you have rather I'd married Jefferson Altman—*boring* Jefferson Altman?" She giggled, enjoying the magic the wine performed on her.

"What about Miles Stafford?"

Destiny frowned. "Why is everyone trying to cram Miles down my throat? We're friends. That's it, end of story."

"Because he reminds you of me?" Adam questioned.

"Y-yes." She lifted her hands to cradle her head. She didn't like the way the room spun mercilessly around her, but blinked in surprise at the sound of Adam's rich laughter. "What's so funny?"

His eyes focused on her. "You are. You were never a great liar," he said, shaking his head.

Destiny, no longer trusting her legs to support her weight, moved over to the sofa and unceremoniously plopped down.

"Desi," Adam said, moving to stand in her line of vision. "Open your heart and see the gift that's standing before you before it's too late."

The telephone rang and Destiny jerked to its loud, invasive sound. "Go away," she moaned, mainly because she wasn't in the mood to get up and search for the handheld unit.

"Adam, could you…?" She looked around. "Where did you go?" Frowning and expelling a breath, she shook her head. Adam was dead and she was sitting in her living room, talking to herself.

"Girl, you're definitely losing it," she huffed and pushed up to stand on her wobbly legs. She retrieved the now-empty bottle of wine from the floor and stumbled in a crooked line to the kitchen to search for a new bottle.

Miles glanced at his watch, while returning his cell phone to his hip. He was instantly besieged with worry. He'd been waiting with their new client for Destiny for well over an hour.

"Should we reschedule?" Mr. Michaels, an elderly gentleman with wiry salt-and-pepper hair frowned with his inquiry.

"No, that won't be necessary," Miles assured him. "I'm sure something important must have delayed my partner. Let's just go ahead with our meal and I can fill Ms. Brockman in on the details later." He smiled and suffered through horrible images of the different possibilities that had delayed Destiny. It was just not like her to pull a no-show.

Destiny's creed—wine is fine, but there's not a damn thing that old Jack Daniels couldn't fix—was under review. She didn't have many self-indulgent pity parties—and it was a good thing, too. For, at the moment, she was enjoying the wonderful feel of the toilet's cold porcelain against her face.

What she wouldn't give to have Miles famous hangover remedy that he'd often bragged about. She drew in a deep, shaky breath, and hugged the toilet tighter as a wave of Chinese food and booze gushed and splashed into the bowl.

When the room's spinning accelerated, she was startled by the unexpected feel of something cool pressed against her head and then, just as suddenly, she was weightless and floating in the air. She giggled and waved her arms blithely over her head.

"Watch it. You're going to gouge out my eyes," a deep, familiar voice warned her.

Destiny jerked her head up in a lame attempt to bring her surroundings into focus, but the quick motion caused her stomach to protest violently and a second serving of dinner spewed forward.

"Damn it, Desi," the male voice barked.

She apologized instantly to the voice, but felt another wave overtake her just before her intoxicated world faded to black.

When Destiny came to, it was to the sound and feel of warm water coursing around her body. She moaned and a fuzzy figure leaned over her and called her name. She opened her mouth to speak, but her mouth was as dry as the Sahara and her tongue had transformed into en engorged, leathery monster that made speech impossible.

She heard a loud exhalation before the figure said, "You gave me quite a scare, Desi."

"Adam?" she asked, but the question sounded more like a grunt to her ears.

"What were you trying to do, kill yourself?"

Her moan was her answer to the ridiculous question mainly because the effort to talk took too much out of her.

"Here, swish this," the voice instructed.

She opened her mouth obediently. And instead of the expected taste of water, came the powerful taste of Listerine. She went to spit it out, when the same command was barked at her.

"Swish!"

Grudgingly, she did as she was told then spit the foul-tasting mouthwash back into the Dixie cup he'd provided. Seconds later, the cloud of confusion parted and she realized that her concerned stranger was actually bathing her.

An alarm sounded in her head and she pushed weakly at the pair of soothing hands.

"It's all right. It's all right, Desi."

She relaxed at the sound of the loving nickname Adam had given her. She'd even managed a weak smile as she said his name.

"Desi, Adam's dead. It's me—Miles."

"Miles," Destiny repeated, still smiling. "Sweet, caring, Miles."

He chuckled. "Maybe Wes is right—I've lost my touch."

Lifting a wet hand, Destiny caressed the side of his face. "You're so good to me," she whispered. His blurry features slowly came into focus and her smile grew even wider. "What are you doing here?"

"I'm doing what I've always done—look after you." As he said this, he rubbed a soapy towel over her shoulder. "You were a mess when I found you in here."

"Is that all?" she asked suggestively with a lopsided grin. She lowered her hand to his bare chest. "And the fact that you're not wearing anything is because—?"

One side of his mouth lifted with mild amusement. "I'm not naked. I took off my shirt because you decided to launch your dinner all over it."

"Likely story," she said with a loud, disbelieving laugh. She encircled his neck with both arms, and sat up to press her wet body against his muscular chest. "Whatever you say, dream lover." She kissed the lobe of his ear.

"Oh, is that what I am?" He laughed.

"Are you complaining?" She kissed him and enjoyed the feel as, at first, his tensed lips relaxed. A glorious ripple of pleasure swept through her. She moaned again as her mind took flight.

Miles's strong arms dipped into the tub and, in one impressive lift, pulled her wet body out.

She shivered when the room's cold air hit her body.

Ignoring the loud slosh of water, Destiny and Miles's lips refused to part.

Destiny felt a surge of empowerment at hearing the sound of Miles's moans of pleasure. Then again, she'd always enjoyed these wonderful dreams of making passionate love to him. It was the only time when she allowed her mind to act out all the feelings of her heart.

Miles tore his lips from hers and whispered raggedly, "I can't do this."

Disappointment flared her determination and she pressed her body even closer. "Why? Don't you find me attractive?"

"Extremely," he answered in the same husky baritone she'd always loved. He lowered her legs to the floor so she could stand up. He led her to the sink where he prepared her toothbrush and handed it to her.

"Brush," he instructed.

Again, she did what she was told. When she was done, she turned toward him. "Then why won't you make love to me?" she asked, pouting.

He wrapped a bath towel around her. "Because you're drunk. And because *when* I make love to you I want you to remember it."

She kissed the small dimple in his chin. "I'm not drunk—just a little tipsy," she said, and with a flip of her wrist, the towel fell and pooled at her legs. "There's no point in fighting the attraction between us, so why bother?" She rocked back onto the heels of her feet and became fascinated by his taut small nipples jetting out at her. She favored one with a slow lick.

Miles flinched as if she'd burned him, and then settled his large hands on her shoulders. "It's not going to happen. You're drunk." He retrieved the towel from the floor, but she blocked his efforts to cover her nudity. "Please, don't make this any harder than it already is," he pleaded.

She stopped squirming and responded in a sly purr, "I wasn't trying to make it harder. I was trying to make it fun." Her arms encircled his neck again. "Don't we always have fun together?" She smiled at the exquisite feel of his erection straining against his pants. "Well, at least there's one part of you excited to see me."

"You're not playing fair," he said.

Destiny saw longing in his eyes. "Forget fair. Kiss me."

He did as he was told and leaned down to capture a kiss that rocked both of them to their core.

Blissfully, Destiny closed her eyes and allowed his lips to transport her onto lofty clouds of ecstasy. To date, this was the best dream she'd had of Miles. The tingling sensations from his feathery caresses blossomed feelings she was afraid to put a name to.

Again when his mouth withdrew, she experienced another

stab of disappointment. "You're a terrible tease." She sighed and laid her head against his chest. As she listened to his rapid heartbeat, she thought how ironic it was that its pattern matched her own.

"I better get you into bed," Miles said, thickly.

She smiled. Finally, this erotic dream would get started, she thought. She kissed his chest. "Will you be joining me?"

He drew in a deep breath, and then kissed the top of her head. "No."

Instantly annoyed, Destiny slapped a hand against his chest and turned abruptly. She had every intention of storming off, but her brain and her leg muscles weren't in sync and she fell. But, before she hit the floor, a pair of strong arms enfolded her and once again, she was airborne.

"You're just determined to break your neck, aren't you?"

"What do you care?" she sulked, while nestling her head against his chest. "You probably like the idea of getting rid of me."

He laughed. "Now, where did you get a crazy idea like that?"

She drew in a deep breath, but didn't say anything. At the moment, she loved the feel of his arms wrapped around her. They made her feel safe and secure—nothing could ever harm her as long as Miles was around. He'd helped her build a successful law practice, taught her about health and fitness, and even how to enjoy life.

"I'm sorry," she whispered, and then yawned.

He chuckled. "For what?"

"For being drunk."

"Oh, so you're finally admitting it?"

She nodded and tightened her grip around his neck as he continued to carry her. When he laid her down, she recognized the velvet against her skin as her bedspread. She smiled and stretched her arms out to him in invitation. "Lie down with me."

"I don't think that's such a good idea." He folded the comforter over her.

With a deep sigh of contentment, she curled into a fetal position. "Well, can you at least sit with me for a while?" She waited through his loud exhalation, and then smiled again when the bed dipped beneath his weight.

"Just for a little while," he agreed.

Gazing lazily through the mesh of her eyelashes, Miles looked more angelic than human. "I'm so glad you're here," she admitted.

His smile was like Jesus to a child as he brushed a few strands of her hair from her face. "Actually, there's no place I'd rather be."

Chapter 22

Destiny stretched in her bed and half expected to bump into Miles. When she didn't, her eyes fluttered open to the empty space beside her. What a wonderful dream she'd had; she'd been sick and Miles had come to take care of her. Of course, she'd always enjoyed her fantasies of him, but she'd rather die than to admit such a thing to Lu Jin.

She smiled and adjusted her head against the pillow. What would it be like to actually wake up next to Miles, she wondered. The thought caused her smile to broaden. She'd never thought it possible when she'd first met him, but she truly believed now that Miles would make some lucky woman a great husband.

In the years that they'd become friends, he'd shown her such kindness and tenderness.

She sat up in bed, peeled back the bedspread and was surprised at how cool the room was. Scooting to the edge, she swung her legs over the bed and stood up.

When the room tilted, she quickly remembered the bottles of wine and Jack Daniels she'd guzzled down. "Bad idea to mix liquor," she mumbled and plopped back onto the bed.

She drew in a deep breath and struggled to control the spinning in her head. With her eyes closed, a wicked shiver coursed through her as visions of her and Miles in a bathtub came to mind.

Deciding against another attempt to get out of bed, she reached for the bedspread and huddled again beneath its warmth all the while keeping her thoughts focused on Miles.

For every reason she had for pursuing a relationship with him, there was another preventing it. For example, if things didn't work out between them, it could cost them their partnership. Their partnership! She bolted upright.

"The meeting!" Her gaze darted over to the clock and she moaned miserably at seeing it was three a.m. "I don't believe it." She scrambled out of bed. As she rushed to find her robe, she paid no attention to the baby-blue bath towel that fell to her feet.

Her robe wasn't in the adjoining bathroom and she thought to check the laundry room. Naked, she sprinted out of her bedroom, but stopped dead when she reached the living room and came within inches of smacking into Miles.

His eyes twinkled as he smiled and said, "Well, I guess you're up."

Her mouth fell open and a shriek of horror burst form her lungs as she made an about-face and dashed to her bedroom—which she reached in a time that would have been the envy of any Olympic sprinter.

She slammed the door and fell back against it as she heaved in big gulps of air. *What the hell is Miles doing here?*

"Desi?" Miles questioned through the door.

Her heart plunged to her knees while her mind raced with questions with no answers.

"Destiny, are you all right?" he probed, and she felt the doorknob turn against the small of her back.

"I—I'm fine," she answered. Her eyes darted around for something to put on.

He tried the door again. "Then let me in," he ordered with concern edging his voice.

Images of her wanton behavior in the bathroom flashed from her memory and shame burned her face as she closed her eyes and moaned, "I thought you were a dream."

The knob stopped twisting, but she wasn't fooled into believing that he'd moved away from the door.

"I take it you've sobered up, then?" Miles asked.

Her eyes narrowed suspiciously. Had there been a hint of laughter in his voice? "This is not funny, Miles," she snapped, her embarrassment dissolving into anger.

"On the contrary. I think this is very funny. By the way, nice backside you got there."

At the sound of his rumbling laughter, Destiny kicked the door with the back of her heel. "Stop being an ass!" She bolted away from the door and over to the chest of drawers and found a long flannel nightgown to put on.

"An ass—me?" Miles continued to carry on the conversation from the other side of the door. "A few hours ago you said I was sweet and caring."

She jerked open the door and glared up at him. "Yeah, well, a few hours ago I was drunk."

"And horny," he added with a smirk, then noticed her outfit. "What—no Victoria's Secret?"

Her mouth dropped open, but her larynx choked off any hopes of a snappy comeback line.

"That's okay. You know how I feel about flannel." Miles pushed her chin up to close her mouth. "I don't believe it. Something has finally rendered you speechless."

"Oooh!" She smacked him on the chest and stormed past him. "I want you to leave."

He followed her. "Why, because you're embarrassed? Give me a break. Nothing happened."

"That's not the point," she said, still storming toward the front door. "Something *could* have happened because I was intoxicated and believed that you were just a dream."

He rushed in front of her, just before she reached the door, and blocked her path. "Which means you must have erotic fantasies about me pretty often, huh?" He crossed his arms and stared down at her.

"It was the alcohol," she insisted.

He smirked and looked as if he wasn't buying it. "Then I guess it was lucky for you that I didn't take you up on your offer, isn't it?"

"Leave!"

He tossed up his hands, but still appeared to be amused about the situation. "Fine, fine. Lord knows I don't want to be anywhere I'm not wanted. Our clothes are in the dryer, you can just give mine to me in the morning," he said, turning toward the door.

Fear clutched her heart. She grabbed his arm to prevent him from turning way. "I thought you said nothing happened?"

He laughed. "It didn't, unless you want to count your transformation into Regan from the Exorcist." At her deepening look of horror, he relented in his teasing and pulled her stiff body into his arms. "Look, Destiny. I was worried about you when you didn't show up for our meeting with Mr. Michaels, so I came to check on you. You were sick and I took care of you. I swear that's all that happened."

She relaxed and shook her head against his chest. "I'm sorry. I know you'd never take advantage of me like that. I'm more embarrassed than angry."

Miles kissed the top of her head. "I know that, too. Would you like for me to make you some coffee?"

Sighing, she allowed herself to be grateful for his presence. "That would be nice."

He gave her a tight hug, and then headed toward the kitchen. "Black, right?"

"You know me so well," she said, smiling. She watched as he disappeared into the kitchen before she drew in a breath and exhaled it in a long weary sigh.

A few minutes later, the apartment was enriched by the aroma of freshly brewed coffee. Destiny collected herself and joined her good friend in the kitchen. But the wonderful sight of Miles rustling around with his muscled chest exposed had a heady effect on her.

She eased onto a stool at the breakfast bar with a subtle smile hugging her lips.

Miles caught a glimpse of her smile as he poured her coffee. He set the cup in front of her, and then braced his weight with his hands as he leaned toward her. "I'm glad to see you're in a better mood."

"Well, a girl could easily be spoiled by such good service."

He lifted an inquisitive brow. "Any girl or just you?"

Blushing, Destiny thought it was safe to give an honest answer. "Probably just me."

The smile he gave her made his eyes twinkle. "That's good enough for me."

She laughed and took a sip of her coffee. "Mmm. This is good. Thanks."

"You're more than welcome," he said, and then watched as she sipped at the hot liquid. "Mind if I ask you a question?"

"You just did," she teased, lowering her cup. "But you can ask me another if you'd like."

His beautiful eyes settled on her with an intensity she'd

only witnessed with him in courtrooms. "What's going on with you?"

She shifted uneasily in her seat and pretended to misunderstand his meaning. "My head is spinning and my stomach hurts, other than that—nothing."

His gaze refused to leave her. "You know that's not what I meant."

"I know." She lowered her gaze as she took another sip.

"I saw some newspaper clippings in the living room while you were sleeping," he went on.

Destiny closed her eyes and felt her emotions tremble with fear of exposure.

Miles continued, "Your brother's suicide still haunts you, doesn't it?"

She drew in a deep breath and struggled to respond. "I—I really don't want to talk about this right now." She opened her eyes and looked pleadingly at him.

Miles nodded, but looked disappointed in her answer.

"It's just painful for me," she added.

"It's painful for me to see you do this to yourself," he said. His eyes again locked on her. "I've never seen you like that before and to be honest with you, it scared me."

Destiny read nothing but concern in Miles's expression and in his voice, and she was more than touched by it. She weighed her reasoning for not sharing this particular part of her life with him and concluded that it was time she did.

"Come on. Let's go sit in the living room. This may take a while to explain," she said, picking up her cup.

Miles poured himself a cup and followed her to the living room where her precious newspaper clippings still lay on the table.

Destiny settled on the sofa and Miles sat next to her.

"Adam and I had always been close. I've read studies of how some people suspect that twins share a certain bond.

Their emotions are somehow connected." She braided her fingers for emphasis. "You know what I mean?"

Miles nodded.

"Well, I've always thought it was true—especially when it came to Adam and I. In fact, we used to tease each other about it all the time. Like, he would call me just when I was reaching for the phone to call him—that sort of thing." She exhaled from nearly saying all of that in one breath. "Which is why I can't understand how I didn't know about the strain he was feeling at his new job—or the fact that he was feeling depressed about anything." She shook her head and looked over at Miles.

"I should have picked up on it. But no matter how many times I replay those final days in my mind, I still come up empty. Every time I saw him, he was smiling and seemed more concerned about things that were going on in my life than in his own. I don't know—maybe that should have been my clue. He never talked about himself." She sipped at her coffee, her mind still wandering in yesteryear.

When Miles spoke, his clear baritone voice pulled her back to the present. "You've got to let the past go, Desi."

She smiled and closed her eyes. "My brother used to call me that."

Miles leaned over and set his coffee down on the table. "Did he now?"

She nodded. "There's a lot you do that reminds me of him." She set her coffee down, as well, and continued to shake her head. "I just can't get over how much I miss him."

Miles opened his arms and she slid comfortably into their folds. He held her while her tears trickled on his chest. He kissed the top of her head and murmured softly against her ears of how everything was going to be all right.

Destiny tilted up her head and stared into his eyes. "Thanks for being here for me tonight. I really appreciate it."

He didn't respond, instead his gaze lowered to her lips.

She didn't bother to question the feelings she was experiencing, but gave in to the magnetic force that pulled her forward.

Their lips sealed in a tender passion that caused Destiny's heart to beat in double-time as she melted against him. A moan escaped her at the gentle invasion of his tongue. Soon, she was consumed with the taste of him and she eagerly participated in the ancient dance their tongues performed.

Miles leaned forward to lay her flat on her back against the cushiony sofa. And even through the thick material of her flannel nightgown, the fire of his touch branded her.

His lips withdrew, but it took her a moment to desert the lofty clouds inside her head and open her eyes.

His lucid hazel eyes were focused on her. "I want to make one thing perfectly clear," he said. "I'm not Adam. I'm the man who's in love with you."

Chapter 23

Destiny stared into Miles's eyes while "The Man in Love With You" floated inside her head. It occurred to her a few heartbeats later that she should respond, but she didn't trust herself to speak.

Miles's head dipped and his lips once again pressed against hers. During the midst of their deep sensuous kiss, the word "love" resonated in her heart. He loved her. He'd said so himself—or had he?

Destiny was suddenly suspicious of this whole night. Was she in the middle of a dream? Maybe it was one where she kept waking, but never truly did.

Miles's strong hands inched up her body, and her breath thinned with anticipation. He ended the kiss long enough to pull the gown over her head. And when she lay naked beneath him, a desire to please him engulfed her.

When he leaned over her, his bare chest brushed against her taut nipples and pleasure swept all the way to her toes.

Her eyes drifted to half moons while the thrill of his soft moans throbbed in her ears.

"I love you, Destiny," he whispered, and then reclaimed her lips.

His fingers slid downward, grazing her flat stomach, her firm thighs, and then dipped into the warm, moist passage between her legs.

Destiny gasped, while Miles's kiss became urgent and hungry.

Miles wanted to pace himself, but his hands and body acted as if they held their own agenda. His lips moved from her glorious mouth to nibble on the lobe of her ear.

Blood roared in his head as fire raged wildly in his veins. He hardened at the feel of the erotic rhythm she'd adopted in response to his probing fingers.

Destiny trembled as jolt after jolt of wild orgasmic pleasure rocketed through her while Miles's mouth continued to burn a hot trail between her breasts. With each peak, his tongue teased and flicked before drawing the nipple hard into his mouth.

Slowly, Destiny managed to pull herself from the whirlpool of sweet oblivion to look into the face of the man who'd claimed to be in love with her and she wondered weakly what was preventing her from repeating the same to him.

As if sensing her withdrawal, Miles deserted her breasts to hover over her. "Do you want me to stop?" he asked, in a thick, hoarse whisper that sounded nothing like his usual cool baritone.

No matter what she was feeling, she wasn't about to tell him to stop—she was nowhere near *that* crazy.

"N-no," she whispered, and reached to unbutton his trousers.

He laughed softly. "Here, let me help you with that," he said. In no time, he was relieved of his clothing.

Destiny was fascinated by his size. Her fantasies had paid him a disservice.

Finally, she dragged her gaze away to look up into his twinkling eyes.

"If you tell me to stop now, you'll definitely be off my Christmas card list," he said, producing a condom and putting it on.

She laughed and wrapped her arms around him as his mouth once again devoured hers. His hands returned to their sweet assault across her breasts, and she moaned softly when his mouth retraced the path his hands had taken.

She twisted breathlessly beneath his gentle caresses, and then gasped with exquisite pleasure as he plunged full length into her welcoming softness.

Lost in an incoherent passion, Destiny was consumed by the fullness of him. And when Miles moved inside of her, she ceased to think at all—she just responded to his every touch and movement.

Their breathing came hard and fast as something glorious unfolded within her and spread like a warm fire that grew with each stroke until it was racing in roaring fury.

She twisted fitfully on the cushions and arched greedily to meet his plunging thrusts.

Miles held her hips, while his mind teetered precariously over blissful insanity. Everything about her was new to him—from the way her warm body massaged him to this growing need to possess her. Never had he felt this way about another woman.

A cry of ecstasy tore from Destiny's lips as a volcano erupted inside of her. Miles thwarted the cry with his mouth and held her until her tremors subsided.

It took Destiny a while, but she slowly regained control of her breathing and half expected the alarm clock to jar her awake. However, after a few minutes, the only sound she heard was their labored breathing.

"You could kill a man," Miles whispered against her ear, then shifted to slide next to her.

"Any man or just you?"

He laughed warmly. "Probably just me."

Smiling, she turned in the curve of his arm. "I guess that's good enough for me."

He kissed her forehead, the tip of her nose and then the soft petals of her lips. "God, you taste so good," he whispered before capturing another long kiss.

Destiny welcomed the kiss, mainly because it was a wonderful substitute for the inevitable talk about this drastic change in their relationship.

With an impressive maneuver, Miles shifted, gathered Destiny and stood from the sofa.

She broke the kiss and looked around.

"Cramped quarters," he answered the unspoken question. "It's a shame to let the bed in your room go to waste, don't you think?"

"Good point." Laughing, she slid her arms around his neck as he carried her to the bedroom.

Later that morning, Violet and Adele arrived separately at their children's building, and then bumped into each other at the elevator bay on the first floor. They laughed when they spotted one another, and then hugged in greeting.

"Here to see Miles?" Adele asked, withdrawing from her dear friend.

"Of course." Violet gently pulled at the fur collar of her jacket. "He's supposed to be helping me shop for a new car. The Lincoln keeps having computer glitches—I swear, these modern cars are more trouble than they're worth." She waved a jeweled hand at her friend. "I just want something that faithfully turns over when you twist the key in the ignition. Is that too much to ask?"

"I hear you, Vi." Adele laughed as they stepped into the

elevator. "Destiny and I are going to catch up with Lu Jin and do a little more house shopping."

"Sounds like fun," Violet chirped.

Adele nodded. "It was in the beginning, but we've been looking for four months and now it's about as much fun as watching paint dry."

The elevator bell sounded and the ladies arrived on the fourteenth floor.

Destiny's head reared back as she assumed the top position and rocked hard against Miles, all the while relishing the way he completely filled her.

With his hands firmly on her sides, Miles pumped his hips, wanting desperately to reach the rapturous explosion that lay just beyond his reach.

When the doorbell rang, neither of them paid it any attention because both were on a mission that refused to be compromised.

However, when Adele's voice floated into the apartment, all bets were off.

"Destiny, are you home?"

"My mother!" Destiny's eyes grew wide as she leaped off Miles, snatching the top sheet with amazing speed and agility.

"Destiny?" Adele questioned again.

"I swear, I'm taking back everyone's key to my apartment. This is getting ridiculous."

Miles chuckled. "If you'd done that, last night would never have happened."

She flashed him a warm smile and said, "Good point."

Adele frowned, worried that she'd got the time wrong. She walked back to the front door with the sudden thought that maybe Destiny had slipped over to Miles's apartment for something.

She opened the door and was surprised to see Violet still standing across the hall.

"Can you believe this?" Violet exclaimed. "He's not home."

"Apparently, neither is Destiny," Adele said. "Do you have a key to his apartment?"

"Are you kidding? That boy guards his privacy like the CIA."

"Well, come on over here. I'm sure wherever they've run off to they'll be back soon."

Violet shrugged and crossed the hall to join her friend. "Thanks, I really appreciate this."

Miles propped up on the jumbo pillows against the bed's headboard and watched in amusement as Destiny scrambled for something to put on. "Where is that damn robe?"

"In the dryer," Miles answered still smiling.

Her gaze cut to him. "I'm so happy you find this amusing. Maybe I should let her come back and find you in here."

Miles's brows wiggled at her as his hands slid behind his head. "Fine with me. I have nothing to hide."

Her eyes lowered to slide over his naked form and couldn't believe that she was actually considering jumping back in bed with him.

"See anything you like?" he asked, laughing.

She rolled her eyes heavenward and turned back to the task at hand. "Maybe it's slipped your mind that our mothers are good friends and if my mom finds out about this, so will yours."

Still indifferent, he shrugged; but his eyes narrowed on Destiny and it occurred to him for the first time that while he had confessed words of love last night, he'd yet to hear the same endearments from her. He stiffened at the realization.

"Then Lu Jin and Wes would be next on the list," she went on to say, finally pulling out a pair of sweatpants and a T-shirt.

"I see," he said, as he looked around for his clothes, feeling the full force of his stupidity. How on earth had he allowed this to happen? He moved to sit on the edge of the bed, with a sudden need for air—but there was one thing preventing him from leaving.

Violet and Adele chatted away as they moved into Destiny's living room when Adele's attention was drawn to a discarded gown. She picked it up at the same time Violet discovered a pair of pants.

Simultaneously, their gazes flew to one another.

"Maybe, this isn't a good time to be visiting," Adele said, coloring with instant embarrassment.

"I wouldn't say that." Violet smiled.

Adele frowned, the meaning lost on her.

Violet held up the pants, and then retrieved a nearby pair of boxers.

"Violet, put those back," Adele snapped, appalled.

Instead, Violet laughed after further inspection of the boxers. "I think we just stumbled over a big secret."

Adele was beginning to suspect her friend had gone mad, when Violet spoke again.

"These belong to my son."

Chapter 24

"Destiny?" Adele called out from the living room. "Are you here?"

Destiny raced to her bedroom door and poked her head out and yelled down the hall. "I'm coming. Give me a few minutes. I'm going to jump into the shower." She slammed the door closed and turned to look at Miles. "You stay right there. I think I can handle this," she said, grabbing her selected outfit and rushing into the bathroom.

Miles shrugged. "As you wish."

After a record-breaking shower, Destiny swept into the living room. Her sweatpants and T-shirt clinging to her wet body as though she'd jumped into the water fully dressed. "Mom," she greeted, breathlessly with her eyes shining, but her wide smile diminished when her gaze shifted to Violet. "Mrs. Stafford." She blinked in surprise.

Violet, on the other hand, brightened like a ray of sunshine. "Good morning, Destiny. How are you?"

Heat crept into Destiny's face as a swarm of butterflies

filled her stomach. "Huh? Uh, I mean, I'm doing good." She nodded for emphasis and worried like hell that one of them had mind-reading capabilities, or worse, could see through walls—mothers did, after all, possess unexplained powers.

"That's good, that's good," Violet said.

Silence hung like a death sentence over the three women, before Destiny finally asked, "So what brings you two here?"

Her mother's brows shot up in surprise. "We're supposed to go look at those houses you printed from the internet, remember?"

"Houses?" Destiny repeated dumbly, but then her brain jump-started. "Oh, the houses!" She exhaled in a rush of relief, and then admitted laughingly, "I'd forgotten."

The women smiled.

But that didn't explain why Violet was there. Her confusion must have shone in her expression because Violet suddenly perked up and answered the unspoken question.

"Oh. I, uh, was just waiting for Miles—"

"He's not here," Destiny interrupted.

Violet blinked, and then smiled. "No. I suppose he's not." She met and held Destiny's gaze.

At that moment, a loud thump came from the bedroom.

Destiny's heart leaped into her throat as she jerked in the direction of the sound.

"What was that?" Adele asked.

Eyes wide, Destiny swiveled back to face them with her mouth open for a convenient lie, but no words came to her rescue.

Adele's brows rose inquiringly. "Yes?"

"I don't know. M-maybe I should go check it out," Destiny said, but didn't immediately move.

"Ooo-kay," Adele said, waiting.

Flashing another smile, Destiny turned and dashed to her bedroom.

* * *

Adele and Violet snickered behind Destiny's back.

"I think we should leave them alone," Adele whispered.

Violet's smile turned smug. "Are you kidding? I say we make them squirm."

Destiny flew into her bedroom and slammed the door behind her. "What on earth are you doing in here?" she whispered through clenched teeth.

Wearing a towel draped around his hips, Miles hopped on one foot. He frowned and hissed back. "I stubbed my toe on the nightstand. Is that all right with you?"

"No, it's not. They heard you back here."

"They?" Miles lowered his foot, but continued frowning. "Who's all out there?"

"Our mothers!"

"*My* mom is here?" Miles asked in disbelief.

"Yes." Destiny flailed her arms. "It's like they have a damn radar gun on us or something."

"Well, I don't know about your mother, but that's definitely a possibility with mine," Miles said. "Did she say what she was doing here?"

Destiny paced nervously. "She said she was waiting for you."

"Oh." Miles slapped his forehead and rolled his eyes heavenward. "I forgot. I'm supposed to take her car shopping."

"Well, she's out there waiting for you. Any ideas on how we get you out of here without them seeing you?"

Miles drew a blank and shrugged.

Destiny moaned and shook her head. "I was afraid of that."

"I got it." He snapped his fingers. "Tell her you just called me and I'm out with Wes and, uh, I told you to tell her to go on to the car dealership and I'll meet her there within the hour." He brightened as if it was an ingenious plan.

"You want me to lie to her?" she asked in mild shock, not daring to tell him that she'd already lied to her once.

"Fine, then. Tell her I'm back here, waiting for you to get rid of them so we can finish what we started."

Destiny picked up a pillow from the bed and flung it at him.

Miles ducked and came up smiling. "Look, we can't have our cake and eat it, too."

She huffed and squeezed her forehead as if she'd suddenly developed a headache.

"Do you have a better plan?" he asked, sitting on the bed.

"Of course I do. I just like biting my nails for fun."

"Well, at least hand me my pants so I can stop parading around like this," he said, returning his gaze back to his injured foot.

"What pants?"

Miles's head jerked back in her direction. "You didn't get my pants from the living room?"

Destiny's eyes widened as the blood drained from her face. "I—I didn't think…" She turned toward the bedroom door, suddenly afraid to go back out of it. "They may have already seen them."

"Wait, wait." He came around the bed and over to her. "Let's not panic. Maybe they haven't seen my pants…and boxers. Where was my mother when you went out there?"

"Standing behind the sofa," she admitted, then covered her mouth with her hand and mumbled, "They know."

"Now, calm down. You don't know that for sure."

"Come on. They've been here at least fifteen minutes. Surely, they've gone to sit down in the living room by now." She started pacing again. "Damn, damn, damn."

"We're not going to get anywhere panicking."

Destiny turned angry eyes toward him. "I know that you're

trying to be the voice of reason but, quite frankly, you're riding my last nerve."

Miles held his hand up in surrender. "I was just trying to help."

Destiny drew in a deep breath, and then headed for the door.

"What are you going to do?" Miles asked.

She turned toward him, with a blank expression. "I'm going to wing it. Wish me luck."

Now he drew a deep breath, as well. "Good luck." He watched her as she slipped out of the door before adding, "Because you're going to need it dealing with my mother."

"It was nothing," Destiny informed Adele and Violet, who were sitting at the breakfast bar, when she returned. "Just a book fell from the nightstand."

As they sipped from the steaming coffee cups, the women's gazes rose to meet her.

Destiny relaxed at the thought there was still a chance they hadn't gone to sit in the living room yet. She chanced a nervous glance over into the living room and saw Miles's clothes in a pile by the coffee table.

"Destiny?" Her mother's voice caught her attention.

She jerked her gaze back to them. "Yes?"

"I was asking you what book you were reading?"

"What book?" Destiny asked, her mind drawing a blank.

Adele blinked. "The book that fell in your room—anything good?"

Destiny blurted out the first thing that came to mind. "The Bible," she lied.

"The Bible," Adele repeated, and then looked to Violet.

Great, Destiny thought, *I am going to hell for this one.* "Yeah, just figured it was about time I, uh, read it."

Violet and her mother just nodded with barely suppressed

smiles. Probably, Destiny guessed, because they didn't buy the lie.

"By the way." Destiny thought it was best to change the subject so she launched right into another lie. "I just called Miles on his cell."

Violet lifted a delicate arched brow. "Oh?"

"Uh, yeah." Destiny cleared her throat. "He's out doing something with Wes and he asked that I tell you to go ahead on to the dealership and, uh, he will meet you there in about an hour."

Violet held her gaze for what seemed like, to Destiny, an eternity before she finally smiled and asked, "Did he now?"

Destiny swallowed hard and nodded. In her mind, she could smell and hear the fires of hell roaring toward her.

Adele lowered her head and sipped her coffee.

Destiny's heart dropped when she thought for a fleeting moment that she'd actually seen a smile hugging her mother's lips.

Violet, on the other hand, drew in a deep breath and gave Destiny a wide, beautiful smile. "Well, isn't that just like Miles to run off with Wes like that? Did he happen to say which dealership?"

"Which dealership?" Destiny repeated, with a rising panic.

Violet nodded. "Yes. We'd talked about several models yesterday and couldn't decide on a Lexus or a Mercedes."

Destiny stared, and then picked one herself. "Lexus—I believe."

Though Destiny would've thought it impossible, Violet's smile brightened.

"Excellent choice, my dear," Violet said, winking. She took another sip of her coffee and stood from the bar. "Then I guess I better get a move on if I plan to catch him."

"I'll go down with you," Adele suggested. "I think I left something in my car." She looked at Destiny. "You're going to need a few minutes to get ready, aren't you? Or are you going dressed like that?"

"Oh—yeah." She smiled. "It's going to take me at least a half an hour."

"Take your time. In fact, I'll just run a few errands and come back," Adele said, still smiling. She turned and walked with Violet to the door.

Destiny followed demurely, relieved to get rid of them so easily. But victory slipped through her fingers when Violet turned around.

"Destiny, my dear. When you speak to Miles, tell him to hurry and that I'd appreciate it if he take better care of those expensive, silk boxers I bought him for Christmas, and not just leave them lying around your living room." She leaned over, kissed Destiny's cheek and then slipped out the door.

Adele, barely able to suppress her laughter, also kissed Destiny and said, "Take your time. I'll call before I come back."

Chapter 25

Miles stood from the bed when Destiny returned. "Well?" he asked, eagerly.

Despondent, Destiny threw his clothes and hit him squarely in the face. "Your mother asks that you don't leave your boxers lying around the apartment."

Miles's shoulders hunched forward as his mouth dropped open. "You're kidding me."

She plopped down beside him on the bed. "I wish I was." She shook her head and rolled her eyes at the sound of Miles's deep rumble of laughter as it filled the room.

"This isn't funny," Destiny whined miserably. "How long do you think it will be before all our friends know about what happened?"

"What's the big deal if they find out?"

Destiny held out her hand. "For one thing, I don't want everyone thinking that we're an instant couple. Especially, when I haven't had time to think about how I feel about what happened last night."

Miles clamped his jaw shut as her words plunged like a knife into his heart. "Good point." For the first time in his life, he was going to be the recipient of the "let's be friends" speech after a wild night of passionate sex. He felt sick.

Destiny continued to ramble about the consequences of their actions without looking up at Miles. If she had, he was sure she'd have easily read his pained expression.

By the time she did look at him, he had his emotions safely hidden beneath a stony facade.

"You understand what I'm saying, don't you?" she asked.

"Makes perfect sense to me," he said, retrieving his boxers and slipping them on.

Destiny exhaled. "Good. I knew you would. I mean, we don't want to make last night too much of a big deal. And we don't need to involve our friends in what happened, right?"

"Right." He removed the towel, and then grabbed his pants.

She smiled and the sight of her relief only twisted the knife in his heart.

"I better get going," he said.

"Oh," Destiny said. "I told your mother to meet you at the Lexus dealership. I assume you know which one."

He nodded and turned toward the door.

"Hey." Destiny stood and touched his arm. "Are you all right?"

Anger boiled in his blood as he looked at her, but he kept his hard mask in place. "Never better," he responded, his voice devoid of emotion.

Destiny's hand fell from his arm as she studied him.

Not in the mood to be dissected, Miles turned and left her bedroom.

"Something is wrong. Tell me what it is," she said, following close on his heels.

"There's nothing to tell." He kept walking. He went into

the kitchen and continued on to the adjoining laundry room where he pulled his shirt out of the dryer.

"I don't believe you," she said, crossing her arms and blocking his exit from the laundry room.

Miles, however, placed his hands on her shoulders and physically moved her away from the door frame. "I gotta go," he said icily and headed toward the door.

"Miles," she snapped.

He jerked back and faced her. "Tell you what… Why don't you get back to me when you figure out what you want or where you think we should go from here—especially since you've made it clear that my feelings on the matter are moot."

Before Destiny had a chance to respond, Miles turned, wrenched open the door and slammed it behind him.

Destiny felt as if she'd been cast in a bad movie as she stared at the closed door. What had she done? They hadn't been out the bed more than an hour and already they were fighting. She slapped her hand against her forehead. "Stupid, stupid, stupid."

"Stupid, stupid, stupid." Miles entered his apartment with a strong need to throw something. He had never felt so humiliated. Why couldn't he have left last night when she'd asked him—why did he have to play hero in the first place? He collapsed into a nearby chair in the living room and tried to figure out a way to repair the damage to his and Destiny's friendship.

The sound of the telephone ringing was slow to penetrate Lu Jin's dreamy haze. In fact, she'd hoped for a few more hours of sleep before she actually had to get out of bed. But apparently, the caller either had something important to say or didn't have a life.

"Are you going to get that or am I going to have to throw that damn thing across the room?"

She moaned and wished like hell she'd remembered to buy a new answering machine yesterday. She stretched an arm out from beneath the covers and fumbled around the nightstand in search of the hand unit. "This better be good," she said, groggily.

"Lu Jin, it's me, Destiny."

Lu Jin's eyes lifted slightly. "I'm listening."

Just then, another shrill ring filled the bedroom and a groan rose from the covers beside her.

"Lu Jin," Destiny continued. "Something terrible has happened."

Another shrill ring and Wes threw back the sheets and grabbed his cell phone. "Make it fast," he mumbled.

"Wes? This is Miles. Man, something bad has happened."

"What is it?" Lu Jin and Wes asked in unison, and then looked at each other.

"Miles and I slept together."

"Destiny and I slept together."

Lu Jin and Wes pressed their hands over their mouthpieces and looked at each other. "They did it."

"That's great," Lu Jin exclaimed.

"You are the man," Wes encouraged with a wide grin, while simultaneously draping an arm around Lu Jin. "I'm glad you finally took the plunge."

"It's a disaster," Destiny complained in a strained voice.

"Wes, I made a complete fool of myself."

Lu Jin and Wes bolted upright and asked in unison, "What happened?" They looked at each other.

"He left here angry," Destiny said. "I think it's because I said that I wasn't sure where we should go with the relationship. I don't know. I don't know what I was saying. I guess a part of me didn't want him to feel pressured into anything—then again, he told me that he loved me."

"I told her I loved her."

"He said what?"

"You told her what?"

Again, Lu Jin and Wes looked at each other.

"Is someone there?" Destiny asked.

"Did I catch you at a bad time, Wes?"

"N-no, the television is on," they both lied to their friends.

Lu Jin placed her hand over her mouthpiece. "I'll be right back," she whispered to Wes. She climbed out of bed, slipped into her robe and left her bedroom so she could continue the conversation in private. "Now, tell me what happened," she asked, when she'd eased into a chair in the kitchen. "From the beginning."

Chapter 26

Elliott won the four-hundred-dollar pool and decided to treat the gang to a dinner at which Destiny and Miles were the hot topic of discussion.

"Did anyone ever think that when those two finally slept together that our lives would be miserable?" Jared asked, nursing his beer.

"I sure as hell didn't," Wes admitted, sliding an arm around Lu Jin. "This past week, Miles has had a temper out of this world."

"So has Destiny," Lu Jin mumbled. "I mean, that's my girl and all, but she's a walking time bomb."

"Isn't there something we can do?" Debra asked as she slumped back against her seat. "I feel almost responsible for this mess."

"I hear ya," Monique agreed.

Theo stabbed another piece of his steak. "Frankly, I don't think we should be so quick to throw in the towel." With that comment, he successfully grabbed everyone's attention.

"Have you lost your mind?" Lu Jin asked, frowning. "Those two are ready to start World War Three."

He shrugged and chewed his food slowly before responding. "The question you have to ask is why are they mad?"

"Because Miles doesn't want to take things slow," Lu Jin supplied her answer.

"No," Wes corrected, shaking his head. "It's because Destiny has completely ignored my man's feelings."

"What?" Lu Jin's hands flew to her hips and she swiveled to look at him.

"Now don't you two start," Monique piped up and rolled her eyes. "Go on with what you were saying, Theo."

"I was saying that, even though Lu Jin and Wes brought up two good valid points, the problem is much deeper than that. This goes beyond physical attraction—these two are in love with each other."

"Which is exactly what Miles told Destiny," Wes said, his gaze, however, was focused on Lu Jin.

"And Destiny just wants a little more time to analyze her feelings. Why is that such a crime?"

"Because she's had ten years. How much time does she need?" Wes asked.

"Don't be ridiculous," Lu Jin snapped back. "They haven't been sleeping together for ten years."

Juan cleared his throat and grabbed the bickering couple's attention. "Is there something going on with you two that you want to share with the rest of us?"

Lu Jin crossed her arms. "Of course not."

"Not likely," Wes added, shifting in his chair.

But, judging by their friends' suspicious, narrowed gazes, none of them looked convinced.

Embarrassed, Lu Jin suggested, "Can we please get back on the subject of what we're going to do about Destiny and Miles?"

* * *

Destiny was working late in the office. She didn't know how, but somehow she'd managed to get behind in her work. And even as the hours grew late, she realized that she still lacked concentration. It was probably in part because Miles, too, was working late in his office.

In the past week, their working relationship had become just as strained as their friendship. And a large part of her was sorry for that.

She rifled through some more of her paperwork and stopped short when she ran across the list of women she'd made a week ago when searching for Miles's perfect match. A corner of her mouth lifted in amusement. Had that been only a week ago?

At the knock on the door, she jumped as her gaze flew up to meet Miles at her door.

"Here are some of the updated proposals for Mr. Michaels's settlement," he said, entering her office. He crossed the large span of her office, carefully keeping his eyes averted.

Destiny's heart begged her to call a truce to this mess, while her head reminded her that he was the one who'd started this. "Thanks," she mumbled.

Miles dropped the folder on her desk and his eyes caught a glimpse of the title on her notepad: *Finding Mrs. Miles Stafford.*

"What are you doing?" he asked before he could stop himself.

Her eyes followed the direction of his gaze and she was suddenly embarrassed.

"Oh, nothing. This was—"

"You're not still actually thinking about doing that are you?"

"N-no. I just happened to come across this a few minutes ago."

He didn't believe her. "So, you're still looking to pawn me off on someone else. Is that it?"

She frowned. "What are you talking about? This was your idea, remember?"

"That was before we slept together," Miles reminded her. "Oh, I forgot. That doesn't make a difference with you."

Destiny bolted up from her chair. "Now, wait just a minute. I never said anything of the sort."

Miles stepped back, but his blood still boiled in his veins. "You're right. While I was busy pouring my heart out to you—you didn't say much of anything." With that, he turned and stormed out of her office.

Destiny dropped back into her chair. "I'm getting sick of him walking out on me."

Back at his apartment, Miles put his body through the grind in his home gym. He desperately wanted to banish all thoughts of Destiny. But the harder he worked out, the clearer his thoughts and her image became in his head.

He finished with the bench press and sat up. His body was drenched in sweat and he didn't feel any better after having done the punishing workout. It was just as well, he thought, Destiny was probably going to be the death of him. Love. He shook his head, he never saw it coming. Even now, as much as he wanted to hate her, he couldn't.

He reached down and retrieved a discarded towel from the floor and wiped the perspiration from his face. "Maybe I should calm down and just go talk to her," he mumbled to himself.

He stood and carried his troubled thoughts to the shower, where he practiced a speech. "Destiny, we need to talk," he said, and shook his head. He needed a softer approach.

He dipped his head beneath the showerhead, halfway wishing he could wash his jumbled thoughts down the drain. This was probably the most difficult and important thing he'd ever have to do.

Destiny had just finished washing the deep conditioner out of her hair when she heard the doorbell. She twisted a towel around her head and looked at the clock. It was *nearly midnight* and she wondered idly who could be visiting her so late.

Dressed in a two-piece, cotton pajama outfit, she opened her door and was surprised to see Steven Barrett.

"Good evening," he greeted with a broad smile. In his hands he held a bouquet of flowers.

"Steve, what are you doing here?" she asked. Had she forgotten a date or something?

"Actually, I was in the neighborhood when I realized I hadn't heard from you in a while. Did I come over at a bad time?"

It was an odd answer, but she smiled all the same. "No, come on in," she said, reaching up to touch the towel on her head. "I'm sorry you caught me doing my hair."

Steve smiled and waved off her concern. "You look beautiful." He handed her the flowers.

"Thank you. They're beautiful," she exclaimed and inhaled the carnations' scent.

"Sorry, they're not fancy, but they were sort of an impulsive purchase."

"They're perfect. Won't you sit in the living room, while I look for a vase to put these in?"

"Sure," he said and turned in the direction she'd indicated.

She walked away, but before she could disappear into the kitchen, her doorbell rang again.

"Don't worry, I'll get it," Steven told her, since he was closest to the door.

* * *

Miles rocked nervously on his heels as he continued practicing his speech under his breath. When the door flew open, words eluded him at the sight of a grinning Steven Barrett.

Chapter 27

"Miles?"

Miles caught Destiny's voice, but he was already heading back toward his apartment.

"Miles—wait!"

He didn't wait. Instead, he entered his apartment and slammed the door behind him. This time, he did throw something. In a fit of anger, he grabbed a nearby vase and hurled it across the room. Its crash against the wall was a replication of the explosion inside of him.

At the knock on the door, he didn't need a crystal ball to tell him who it was. "Go away!"

Instead, the door flew open and Destiny stormed inside. "I will not go away. This time you're going to talk to me."

Miles turned on her. Even in cotton pajamas and damp hair, she was able to claim his heart. "There is absolutely nothing I have to talk to you about. So please, feel free to return to your prey across the hall."

"I told Steve to leave."

"Well, that makes it all better now, doesn't it?"

Destiny's fists jabbed at her sides as she glared up at him. "Will you shut up? You sound like a complete ass." She shook her head. "What happened between us last week was a mistake. We should have never crossed the line."

Miles clenched his jaw, in part, to prevent himself from spitting fire.

"Just look at us," she demanded. "We went five years without fighting. One weak moment and we can't stand to be in the same room for more than five minutes together."

Miles stepped toward her. "Is that all it meant to you—a weak moment?"

She exhaled. "I didn't mean it like that."

"Sure you didn't," he said coldly. "Are you finished?"

Her eyes glossed with sudden tears. "So you're still not going to talk to me?"

He exhaled in a long, slow breath. "How about I ask you a question instead?"

She straightened and lifted her chin, but her eyes refused to desert his. "Okay."

He moved closer. "How do you *feel* about me?"

"What?" She gave him an incredulous look.

"You heard me." Miles wasn't going to let her off the hook. He was tired of pussyfooting around and he wanted an answer.

Destiny retreated as Miles bore down on her.

"What's the matter—is it a *difficult* question?" he asked. At this moment, even he was surprised by his intense emotions.

"N-no. Yes," she finally admitted. "My feelings for you are complicated."

He stopped. "You're not going to give me some ridiculous crap like you can't separate me from your brother again, are you? Because if you are, what we did last week was illegal in most states." He never saw her move, but her powerful slap jarred him. Panther-quick, he snatched her wrist and held firm.

Destiny responded by slapping him again with her free hand and, just as fast it, too, was seized.

"Fine. You want to know how I feel? I hate you. You're nothing but a selfish ass—"

Miles silenced her with a deep, hungry kiss. The sweet taste and warmth of her mouth was all it took to calm his temper and soothe his soul. In truth, this was all he wanted—to have her in his arms again.

Backed against the front door, he released her hands and pulled her against him. Her breasts pressed against his chest as his mouth took total possession. He didn't want to hear that she hated him. Hell, he didn't want to hear that she liked him. He wanted nothing less than her love. When he'd made love to her, he'd made up his mind that he could no longer settle for being just her friend or business partner.

Miles dragged his mouth from her swollen lips to nuzzle her neck. "Stay with me tonight," he said, raggedly, and braced himself for rejection.

In answer, she curled toward him and reclaimed his lips with a kiss as hungry as his own.

Leaning down, he swung her up into his arms and carried her to his bedroom, where a king-size mahogany sleigh bed awaited them.

Gently, he placed her onto the bed and positioned himself above her. For the past seven nights, he'd yearned for this moment and was afraid that it would never come again. Now that she was there, he planned to savor every kiss and touch as though it was the last.

But as much as he wanted to take his time, their clothes flew off in a flurry of movement.

Moonlight poured through the bedroom windows and illuminated the lovers' bodies.

Miles groaned as he kissed and caressed Destiny and took great pleasure when she shivered and trembled beneath him. Every sound she made heightened his passion and deepened his obsession.

Destiny, meanwhile, floated languorously on lofty clouds of sweet ecstasy and was unable to remember their previous discord. How could her body readily forgive him for his cold behavior toward her this week?

Miles took his time, subjecting her to a slow, delicious torment that threatened Destiny's sanity.

"Miles, please," she begged in a thin, hoarse whisper. Her pride be damned.

"Please what?" he taunted; his lips had moved to pay homage to her sensitive breasts.

Destiny tossed her head back onto the pillows and Miles slid down the bed, his lips and tongue burning a hot trail down her skin.

"Please what, Destiny?" he asked again. His mouth traveled farther south where he gently parted her legs.

Destiny arched and gripped the pillows as tears swelled and slid from the corners of her eyes. She was completely unprepared for the jolts of dizzying pleasure that shot through her—unprepared for her very breath to evaporate from her lungs.

He took his time with this gentle assault and just when she thought she'd die from the sheer ecstasy of it all, her body erupted in a series of explosions while she withered helplessly beneath him.

Miles slid back to hover above her. She could feel him hardened against her. He rained more kisses across her breasts, along her collarbone, and settled into the nape of her neck.

She slid her arms around him, drawing him closer, yet he still didn't enter her.

A dull ache pulsed in the core of her being. As the slow torture continued, the ache became a hard throb, and she felt, once again, her pride leave her. "Miles, please."

"Please what?" he asked in the same teasing tone as before.

More tears slid from Destiny's eyes. "Please, make love to me," she pleaded in a passion-filled voice. She could feel his smile against her neck.

"Are you sure?"

"Dear God, yes," she panted.

He shifted his weight, and effortlessly, smoothly, he slipped on a condom and entered her.

Destiny gasped as her body played a familiar song that only she could hear and soon her hips rocked to its rhythm.

Miles took her in sleek, powerful strokes and the room was filled with their heavy breathing. His heart soared when she called his name in a mindless continuum, but he still ached to hear those three simple words.

His hands moved over the curves of her back, then held firm to her small hips. His pace quickened as his breath hitched and the promise of a glorious release loomed on the horizon.

Destiny clawed at his back as she tensed; her muscles tightened exquisitely around him. He clenched his teeth and gave into the powerful force that rocked and bound them.

When he slumped over her, their breathing still labored, he heard the words his heart longed to hear.

"I love you," she said. She turned her head and kissed him tenderly. "I've loved you for years."

His smile was bright in the moonlight. "I knew it," he said and kissed her back, and then asked, "Now, that wasn't so hard, was it?"

Destiny snuggled closer. "No. I guess not." Her gaze probed his. "When did you first know?"

"Honestly?"

She nodded.

"That night of the blackout five years ago. We spent the night in a room lit with candles and I kept thinking how beautiful you looked."

Playfully, she pushed him away. "Please. I remember that night. I looked like who did it and what for."

Miles chuckled lightly. "Yeah, you were looking a little rough, but that's not what I meant."

She grew warm beneath his gaze. "What did you mean?"

"You were funny, smart, and easy to talk to. But I have to tell you. I was physically attracted to you the first day we met—gay or not."

"Oh, my gosh." She covered her mouth with her hands, and then spoke through the open gaps of her fingers. "I totally forgot about that." She laughed. "That really was a bad joke they played on you."

He laughed along with her. "Yeah, well. You certainly didn't win any brownie points when you pepper-sprayed my eyes."

She lightly hit his chest. "You deserved it and you know it."

"What?"

"You did. I hardly knew you and you'd cornered me in an elevator talking about how you thought I was attracted to you."

His laugh deepened. "When you say it like that, it does sound bad."

"It was bad. It's a good thing you're good-looking, because if you had to depend on your pickup lines, you would be a forty-five-year-old virgin."

His rumble of laughter shook the bed.

Destiny laughed, too, and then leaned over to kiss his chin. "You know I'm right."

"Probably." He tilted her chin up and stole a feathery kiss. "Tell me you love me," he said. "I want to hear it again."

"I love you," she responded without hesitation. "I love you."

This time, his mouth covered hers in a sweet hunger and for the rest of the night they explored every inch of their bodies and their love.

Chapter 28

"Somebody got laid," Lu Jin surmised with a smile.

Blushing, Destiny's coffee cup stopped midway to her lips. She opened her mouth with no idea of a good response.

"Don't bother lying." Lu Jin waved her off. "I know that look."

"What look?" Destiny sipped her coffee and frowned.

Lu Jin shook her head. "You really are lousy at this, aren't you?" She laughed. "Do you realize that you've been humming 'Natural Woman' for the better part of an hour?"

Had she? She hadn't noticed.

"And," Lu Jin went on, "you just put a ton of cream and sugar in your coffee—you always drink it black."

Destiny looked down into her cup and noticed for the first time the hot liquid was a light tan color. "All right. So you caught me."

Lu Jin perked as she wiggled her brows. "Was it with who I think it was?"

Another wave of heat scorched Destiny's face as she bit her lower lip and nodded. "I can't believe what's happening between us."

"Well, thank God for small miracles. Maybe we all can breathe a little easier around you two."

Destiny's brows slanted. "What do you mean?"

"Just what I said. I've been afraid to mention Miles's name around you all week."

"Why?"

Lu Jin rolled her eyes. "You've got to be kidding. I think you called him everything but a child of God after what happened the first time."

"Oh, that." Destiny waved off her observation. "That's over with now. We've talked it through and we decided that we're going to take our relationship to the next level."

"So you guys are officially a couple now?"

"Yep." Destiny nodded.

Lu Jin stood from the bar stool and walked around the counter to hug her. "That's great. I'm so happy for you."

Destiny's gaze drifted. "Yeah, everything's great."

Lu Jin surveyed her friend's expression. "So what's wrong?"

"Nothing," Destiny answered with a flat-line smile.

"Well, you've convinced me." Lu Jin crossed her arms. "Come on, spit it out."

Destiny drew in a deep breath. "The problem is everything *is* so good."

Lu Jin's brows cocked. "You want to run that back by me?"

With shoulders dropped, eyes leveled, Destiny confessed, "I'm afraid to believe in this feeling—I'm afraid that it's not going to last." She waited for her friend to say something cynical, but when she didn't speak, Destiny continued, "It's like I'm expecting at any minute for it all to be snatched away."

"I don't believe it," Lu Jin finally broke through her stupor.

"What?"

With a bark of laughter, she said, "You actually believe in that family curse."

"No, no. That's not it," Destiny emphatically denied, but her protest sounded hollow. She closed her eyes. "I know it's stupid."

Lu Jin exhaled and when she spoke, there wasn't a hint of her previous amusement. "I wouldn't say it was stupid."

Opening her eyes, Destiny's gaze darted to Lu Jin to evaluate her sincerity. "We're talking about seven generations of Stafford men. What would I do if the curse proves true?"

Lu Jin draped her arms around Destiny's shoulders and gave them a supportive squeeze. "Maybe you shouldn't dwell on what-ifs. You could go crazy doing that."

Destiny lowered her head. "How can I do that? When I'm watching him sleep, those questions damn near smother me. And I can't help but feel that we wasted ten years finding our way toward each other."

"Wishing you should have taken him up on his offer in the elevator that fateful day?"

Despite her misery, Destiny laughed. "Not quite."

Smiling, Lu Jin returned to her stool and picked up her coffee cup. "Frankly, I don't think you two would've gotten too far ten years ago—or even five. You were different people." She shrugged. "People change."

Destiny tilted her head and frowned.

"What?" Lu Jin asked.

This time, Destiny shrugged. "I don't know. I get the sense that you weren't just referring to me and Miles."

Lu Jin waved her off. "Don't be silly. Of course I was."

Destiny watched her, but said nothing.

"In my heart of hearts," Lu Jin said, "I think this is your time to be together."

"I hope you're right." Destiny drew in a deep breath. "Because I couldn't handle it if I lost him."

* * *

"To Destiny and Miles," Adele saluted and held up her champagne glass.

"I'll toast to that," Violet heartily agreed as they clinked their glasses together.

"I can't believe it's finally happened—and without our help," Adele marveled. "Or do you think we played a small part in it?"

"As much as I would like to take some credit for this wonderful miracle, I don't think so."

"Too bad," Adele said, disappointed. "I guess at this point it doesn't matter how it happened. So what do you think about a summer wedding?"

Violet drummed her jeweled hand against her chin as she thought about it. "Summer is good, but spring would be better, don't you think?"

Adele nodded. "Yeah, and it would be sooner."

Violet laughed. "And here I was thinking I was being subtle."

"About as subtle as a hammer over the head." Adele laughed. "What about a ceremony at Calloway Gardens?"

"Ooh, nice. But what about on a cruise ship?"

Adele snapped her fingers. "I like the way you think." Then she frowned. "You think Destiny and Miles would be upset with us planning their wedding? I mean, they're not engaged, yet."

Violet waved off her concern. "No sense in splitting hairs. They can thank us later. Besides, I want a wedding as soon as possible and a grandchild nine months later."

"Here, here." Adele raised her glass again.

Miles, drenched in sweat, faked to the right, then turned left and made a beautiful three-point shot into the basketball net. His four-man team erupted in a roar of victory.

Wes mumbled his congratulations.

"Don't look so disappointed." Miles drew in large gulps of air. "You guys haven't been able to beat us in over a year."

Wes glanced at his team of Juan, Zack and Theo and noticed they wore the same bleak expression. "We'll get y'all one of these days," he panted.

Jared slapped Wes hard on the back. "Never give up on your dreams," he said.

Miles's team laughed.

"Everyone's a damn comedian," Wes frowned.

Kyle slapped Wes on the back. "Hey, we get our best material from you guys."

"Ha. Ha." Wes tried to remain sour, but a smile crept across his lips.

"So, lunch is on you guys again," Elliott happily reminded them.

"Hell, you still have money left over from the pool, I say *you* buy lunch."

Miles frowned. "What pool?"

All, except for Wes, looked sheepishly at him.

Miles rolled his eyes. "Never mind, don't tell me."

Wes shrugged. "You just couldn't wait one more night, could you?"

Despite his annoyance, Miles laughed. "Technically, it was close to four in the morning."

Wes's head jerked toward Elliott. "That made it the first of September. Hey, give me my four hundred dollars."

"Four hundred?" Miles asked shocked. "It was that much."

Wes ignored Miles. His gaze remained locked on Elliott. "I want my money."

The other guys laughed.

"You guys are going to have to do lunch without me." He looked at his watch. "I'm having lunch with Destiny today."

Jared smiled. "So you two finally made up?"

Miles's eyes narrowed suspiciously. "Why—was there another pool for that, as well?"

Guilt covered their faces and Miles had his answer.

"You guys are impossible."

"Maybe so," Wes conceded. "But you and Destiny yield a higher return than anything on the stock market. I'll give y'all that much."

"I'll put that in my stack of useless information," Miles replied with a roll of his eyes. "Maybe the next pool should be on what year you finally hook up with Lu Jin."

Theo chuckled. "Now, that's a bet I wouldn't mind getting in on."

All humor faded from Wes's expression as Miles read his friend like an open book.

"You sly devil," he said.

The other men looked at Wes, dumbfounded.

"Mind your own business," Wes warned with a humorless grin.

Miles shrugged. "I'm just following your example."

In a burst of good cheer, the guys pounded Wes's back and congratulated him.

"I should have never doubted your strategy," Theo marveled. "You are definitely the man."

"Whatever," Wes said, as pride seeped into his features.

"I better get going," Miles said, turning to retrieve his gym bag from the side court.

"We'll catch up with you later, man," Zack called after him.

"Sounds like a plan," Miles agreed. Anxious to see Destiny, he hurried to his car. He would be the first to admit that his excitement to see Destiny was a bit strange. After all, there was rarely a day he didn't see her—but this was the first time he could be with her in a sort of silent possession.

He smiled and allowed his thoughts to drift toward the

future. He rolled off the name "Mrs. Destiny Stafford" and liked the sound of it. Why not? It wasn't like they were rushing things. They had known each other for ten years, he reasoned.

Thoughts of Destiny were the reason for Miles's good mood and the reason he ran a red light. A horn blared and Miles looked to his right.

"Dear God, no," he said, seconds before a truck plowed into him.

Chapter 29

When Destiny received the call from Wes, her world tilted on its axis. She remembered screaming, but not collapsing in a heap on the floor. Thank God Lu Jin was still there. She had taken the phone from Destiny's steel grip to speak with Wes.

Snapshots of Miles flashed in Destiny's mind. She remembered vividly the last time she'd seen him, kissed him and made love to him.

"Come on, Destiny," Lu Jin urged. "We need to get over to the hospital."

Destiny remained on her knees—promising the Lord everything, if he would just spare Miles.

"Destiny?" Lu Jin said again. "He's being taken to Grady Hospital. He's not dead…"

Destiny heard the word "yet" even though Lu Jin hadn't said it. Her heart squeezed as tears drenched her face. "I can't," she choked out between sobs. In her mind, she already knew what she'd find once they made it to the hospital. "I can't."

Lu Jin's arms slid around Destiny as she grabbed her friend and held on for dear life.

"It's going to be all right," Lu Jin murmured against her ear.

Destiny shook her head, unable to bring herself to believe her friend's encouraging words. The what-ifs had returned in full force and she suffered something akin to an anxiety attack.

Through it all Lu Jin remained by her side. When she was finally able to pull herself together, Destiny realized that she was wasting precious time feeling sorry for herself. Miles needed her and her place was by his side.

Minutes later, they were zipping through traffic in a rush to get to the hospital.

When Violet ended her call with Wes, she forced herself to remain calm but experienced a strong sense of déjà vu. But her facade didn't fool Adele.

"What is it?" Adele stood from her chair and moved over to her friend.

Violet fought her rising tears and lifted her chin. "I need for you to drive me to the hospital. There's been an accident."

Grady Hospital's emergency room was a whirlwind of activity. And for a long while no one could tell Destiny where Miles had been taken and Destiny thought the wait would kill her. For the time being they were directed to the waiting room.

She asked Wes for the twentieth time if he had called Violet.

"She's on her way," he assured her, and draped an arm around her shoulders.

Lu Jin allowed Destiny to clench her hand.

"How bad was it?" Destiny asked Wes, unable to bear another moment of not knowing.

His hesitation wrenched Destiny's heart.

"I really can't say," he finally answered.

The other guys, still dressed in their sweats and T-shirts, paced in front of her. She wanted to scream and tell them to stop. Their pacing was increasing her anxiety, but she couldn't bring herself to say it.

"Would you like for me to bring you something to drink—some water, perhaps?" Wes asked.

"No, thank you." She looked up at him and for first time noticed the deep lines etched into his features. He'd been Miles's childhood friend—had teased him mercilessly about this silly family curse—and now this.

She smiled and watched helplessly as a tear slid from his eyes.

He jumped from his seat and mumbled, "I got to get some air."

Lu Jin dropped Destiny's hand and stood, then as if in afterthought, she looked down at Destiny.

"It's okay," Destiny assured her. "Go to him. He needs you," she said.

Lu Jin leaned down and kissed the top of her head. "Thanks," she said, and then took off after Wes.

Destiny watched her and wondered how long had she suspected something between them? She closed her eyes and shook her head. Did it matter?

Standing, she walked over to the nurses' station and asked yet again about Miles's status. At least this time, there was some information about him in their system.

"It looks like he's in surgery at the moment," the nurse named Theresa said, without taking her eyes from the computer screen.

Surgery? Destiny's heart slammed against her rib cage. "What type of surgery?"

"I'm sorry, ma'am. I'm not pulling that information up.

I'm sure that one of the doctors will be out here to speak with you soon."

With no other option, she turned away from the station and returned to the waiting room, all the while praying for a miracle.

Violet and Adele arrived at the hospital. Both wore the same stricken expressions. Destiny greeted Miles's mother with open arms and Violet slid into her embrace quietly. Then Adele joined their embrace.

An hour later, there was still no word from the doctors.

"I can't stand this," Destiny said, and then pressed a hand against her mouth. Tears glided down her face as she prepared herself for the worst. Only bad news could take so long, she reasoned.

"I need to get out of here," Destiny finally said and bolted from the waiting room.

"Wait. I'll come with you," Adele said, rushing behind her.

Outside, Destiny inhaled Atlanta's muggy humidity as though it was the finest tropical breeze while tears fell freely down her face.

"Destiny?"

She heard her mother behind her, but she wasn't ready to slip her brave face back on—not yet. "It's all right, Mom. I'm fine," she lied, without turning to face her.

Adele moved next to her and draped a supportive arm around her. "You are far from being all right," she said.

Destiny closed her eyes and pursed her trembling lips together.

"Come on. You can talk to me."

Destiny gave a half laugh and pulled away. "Well, that's a new one," she said, unable to rein in her sarcasm.

"W-what is that suppose to mean?" Adele asked, hurt echoed clearly in her voice.

Destiny faced her. "Don't you remember the last time we were here?"

Adele's face clouded.

"*I* do. I remember it quite well actually. We were here waiting for the final word on Adam. Is this beginning to sound vaguely familiar?"

"Destiny, don't."

"Don't what—talk about Adam? Hell, that should be easy, we haven't talked about him in twelve years. But you know what, Mom? I *want* to talk about him. I want you to know that there's not a day that goes by that I don't miss him. It kills me to know that you blame him for Dad's death."

Adele's usual calm demeanor was shattered and she looked on the verge of tears.

"I'm sorry, Mom," Destiny lowered her voice, regretting her outburst.

"There's no need for you to be sorry," Adele said. "You're just saying how you feel. You should never be sorry for that." She reached inside her purse and removed a tissue.

Destiny stared at her. "How do *you* feel?"

"Ashamed." Adele flashed her a brief smile. "Ashamed because you're right. I did blame Adam for Edward's death. Pain has a way of easing itself when there's someone to blame for it. Unfortunately, I couldn't find anyone to blame for Adam's death. It's sort of a weird cycle I have going inside of my head. It's stupid really." She sniffed and blotted her eyes. "Really stupid."

In that brief moment, Destiny realized what she was doing; she was picking this moment to lash out at her mother to cover up what was going on now. She moved over to her mother and draped her arms around her. "I'm sorry, Mom. I didn't mean to hurt you."

Adele reached up and caressed her daughter's cheek. "And I didn't mean to hurt you all these years."

They stood beneath the portico of the emergency room entrance for some time and when they returned inside, they were puzzled to find the waiting room empty of their friends.

"Excuse me," Destiny said as she once again returned to the nurses' station. "Was there any news on Miles Stafford?"

Nurse Theresa looked at her. "What was the name again?"

"Stafford," she said.

The woman typed in the name, and then winced as she looked back up at her. "It looks like he's been moved to I.C.U.—it doesn't look like he's regained consciousness."

Destiny nearly crumbled to the floor. "May I see him? I believe our other friends and family have already gone back there."

"Just follow the signs leading down that hall and it will take you to I.C.U."

"Thank you." Destiny flashed her a weak and trembling smile. She and her mother turned away and headed in the direction the young nurse had pointed them.

Nurse Beverly returned to her chair and looked over at her coworker Theresa who was solemnly shaking her head.

"What's with you?" Beverly asked.

"That poor woman. She's here to see that shooting victim Miles Stanford up in I.C.U."

Beverly turned and caught a glimpse of the woman just before she turned a corner out of sight. "Humph. I thought she was here to a Miles *Stafford*."

Miles smiled slyly at his family and friends, touched by their concern. "I'm fine, I'm fine," he assured them. "I just have to wear this cast for a while—no big deal."

"You scared me to death." Violet threw her arms around him.

He winced in pain but didn't dare to tell her to loosen her

grip. He made a quick scan of the crowd and grew concerned when he didn't see Destiny.

Lu Jin followed his gaze. "Oh!" She perked up. "We forgot to tell Destiny you were okay. I'll go get her. She's just right outside."

Miles relaxed. "No, that's okay. I'm free to go—I'll get her."

"Well, we better hurry. She was a wreck when the nurses mistakenly told her you were in surgery."

Miles and the gang headed out of the hospital through the emergency room doors, and Miles was puzzled yet again when he didn't see Destiny.

"Well, they were out here a few minutes ago," Lu Jin said.

Miles frowned. "You guys, go ahead on. I'll find Destiny and catch up with you later."

"Are you sure?" Wes asked. "We don't mind waiting."

"I'm not leaving here without you," Violet stated flatly.

"Then you can help me find her," he said. "The rest of you, go on. I'm fine." After a few pats on the back and hugs, Miles was finally free to go and search for Destiny.

Nurse Theresa looked thoroughly embarrassed by her big blunder and informed Miles that she had sent Destiny to I.C.U. for Miles Stanford.

Guessing at the torment Destiny may be going through, Miles and Violet rushed in the direction the nurse had pointed.

Destiny and Adele finally made it to the intensive care unit and asked one of the nurses for Miles's room.

"I'm sorry," Nurse Stacy said, ashen-faced. "Mr. Stanford has passed away."

"What?" Destiny slumped back against her mother.

"I'm sorry, but if you want to talk to Dr. Bradley, he's still talking to the other family members down the hall."

Destiny simply stared at the woman.

"Thank you," Adele said, and turned Destiny away from the nurses' station.

"I don't believe it," Destiny murmured. "He's gone."

"Shh. Now, now." Her mother led her a small group of chairs. Destiny collapsed in one and released a floodgate of tears. Adele pressed her daughter's head onto her shoulder.

"All this time, he knew. He tried to tell us, but we wouldn't believe him." She closed her eyes and wanted to crawl inside herself. "I don't think I can handle this," she said.

"I know it doesn't seem like it right now, but you will," Adele encouraged in a small trembling voice. "Trust me, you will."

Destiny shook her head. "It just isn't fair. There wasn't enough time." She pulled away from her mother and tried to wipe away her tears, but her attempts failed as more tears slid from her eyes. Frustrated, she lowered her head into her hands and wept.

Adele pulled her back into her embrace.

"What am I going to do?" Destiny asked. "I loved him— and I waited too long to tell him."

"Shh, honey. I'm sure he knew."

Miles rushed up the hall, and the sound of a woman's mournful tears reached his ears.

"It's not enough," Destiny sobbed. "I wanted to grow old with him—and have his children."

Miles stopped in his tracks, surprised at what he was hearing.

"I woke up this morning with everything," Destiny went on to say. "Now, I have nothing."

"That's not true, Desi," Miles said. "You still have me."

Destiny and Adele jumped from the chairs and turned around.

"Miles!" Destiny, unable to believe her eyes, raced toward him with her arms opened.

He swept her up into his embrace and spun her around. When he'd finally set her down, he was stunned to see her still crying. "There's no need for these." He wiped at her tears. "I'm here and I'm never going to leave you."

"I'm going to hold you to that." Destiny wagged her finger at him.

"You do that." He kissed her. "You do that."

Violet and Adele drifted toward each other, fresh tears springing from their eyes.

"What do you think about a winter wedding?" Violet leaned over and asked Adele.

"I think that only gives us a couple of months to plan—but it's definitely doable."

And about that curse…

Epilogue

Three years later...

Destiny and Miles returned to Violet's house late in the evening exhausted. So much so, in fact, they collapsed on the sofa instead of journeying upstairs to the guest room.

"What a day," Destiny said, kicking off her high heels and enjoying the instant relief to her feet.

"Tell me about it." Miles yawned and draped an arm around her shoulders to pull her closer.

Violet stuck her head around the corner to peek into the living room. "I thought I heard you two in here." She smiled and entered the room carrying a large box. "How was the wedding?"

"Wonderful...considering." An instant memory of the day's drama popped into Destiny's mind.

Miles chuckled. "At least it wasn't us running around like chickens with their heads cut off."

"Yeah. It was sort of a sweet revenge to see Lu Jin and Wes go through the motions this time. Wasn't it, hon?"

Miles gave her a quick kiss. "Definitely."

"So everything went without a hitch?"

Destiny and Miles looked at each other and laughed.

"We didn't say that," Miles said. "Theo, of course, was one of the groomsmen, but he had gotten drunk the night before and was still suffering a severe hangover. We didn't think he was going to make it down the aisle."

Destiny jumped in. "Lu Jin had a bad case of wedding jitters. For a moment there I really thought she was going to leave Wes standing at the altar."

Miles glanced over at her in mild shock. "Wes nearly did the same thing."

They laughed again.

Violet shook her head as she headed toward the vacant love seat beside the sofa. "Sounds like I missed quite a wedding." She sat down and placed the box on the coffee table.

"The minister was an hour late. The ring bearer tripped and the rings rolled under the pews—that took another thirty minutes to find both rings. And all the while, I had to try and convince Lu Jin that none of this was a sign of their marriage being doomed."

Violet laughed and withdrew a tissue from the table to blow her nose.

Miles frowned. "Your cold hasn't gotten any better?"

Violet blotted her nose. "Actually, I'm starting to feel much better."

"I hope little Miles wasn't too much trouble for you," Destiny said, worrying.

Violet waved off her concern. "Don't be ridiculous. My grandson is always the perfect angel."

The exaggeration made Destiny and Miles laugh again.

"But while he took a nap today, I did do something that

I've been meaning to do for years." She clapped her hands and beamed a smile at them.

"And what's that?" Miles asked.

Destiny laid her head against her husband's chest and slid her arms around his waist while she watched Violet bubble with excitement.

"I cleaned the attic."

Destiny looked up at her husband, struggling not to laugh.

"Well," Miles said with a smile hugging his lips, "sounds like you really know how to let your hair down."

Violet leaned over and popped him on the knee. "Don't patronize me."

Miles continued to smile.

"Like I was saying—I was up in the attic and reminiscing about a lot of stuff that's up there when I came across this box." She pointed to the one on the table. "It has a lot of personal stuff about Richard—things I've never seen before."

Destiny sat up.

Miles leaned forward to bend back as flap of the box to look inside.

"It also has a lot of his Army stuff," she added.

Destiny looked at Miles. "I didn't know your father was in the military."

Miles nodded. "He fought in Vietnam." He shrugged. "Once, he thought if he was going to die young he might as well die fighting for his country."

Destiny shifted, uncomfortable with the conversation drifting toward "the family curse."

"Actually, I don't think this box belonged to your father. I believe it was your grandmother's stuff. I seem to recall when she passed away your father put some of her things in the attic." Violet reached inside the box. "There are a lot of baby pictures and letters written by her. And there are these." She pulled out a small stack of papers.

"What are those?" Destiny asked.

"Adoption papers."

Destiny was confused. "Adoption papers?"

Violet nodded and handed them to Miles before reaching for something else. "And there's this, too."

Destiny took the weathered piece of paper and looked at it. "It's a birth certificate for a Richard Kendall." She looked up at Violet. "I don't understand."

"At first neither did I, but then I started putting things together. I mean about the Stafford curse."

Destiny's apprehension increased. "I thought you said that you didn't believe in the curse."

"I don't." Violet stiffened, but failed to maintain eye contact. "But things sometimes float in the back of your mind."

"You mean like the question of what if you're wrong and there really is a curse?" Destiny asked, knowing exactly what her mother-in-law meant.

Violet's smile wavered at the corners. "I'm sure you two have dealt with the same questions."

"Only all of my life," Miles answered, unable to keep the sarcasm out of his voice.

"But don't you see? This settles it for once and for all." Violet inched closer to the edge of her seat. "If these papers are legitimate, and I don't see any reason why they're not, then you're not susceptible to the Stafford curse because you're not a true Stafford—neither was your father. And according to that birth certificate, Richard was actually older than he thought."

Miles blinked, and then stared back down at the papers he held.

Destiny's heart bloomed with hope.

"But Dad died," Miles tried to vocalize his jumbled thoughts.

Violet's expression softened. "We're all going to die, sweetheart. But Richard's death had nothing to do with a curse. It was an accident—nothing more, nothing less."

Destiny and Miles digested this information and looked at each other. The revelation remained on their minds well after they'd checked on Miles Junior and retired for the night.

"So what do you think?" Destiny asked, easing comfortably into the crook of his arm.

"It's a lot to take in," he admitted honestly. "I wonder why my grandmother never told my father that he was adopted or if she had why he had never told us."

Destiny nodded and watched her husband's frown deepen. She reached up and kissed him gently.

Miles savored her lips and when she broke away, he smiled down at her. "What was that for?"

"Do I have to have a reason?"

He turned and pulled her pliant body toward him. "Then I guess I don't have to have a reason to do some things to you, either."

She giggled and pulled away. "You better not. Your mother is in the next room. We can wait until we return to our own bed tomorrow night."

He chuckled and nibbled on her ear. "I'm sure she's fast asleep."

Destiny's body melted at the feel of his warm breath against the nape of her neck. All thoughts of a curse vanished. And on their tenth, twentieth and thirtieth wedding anniversaries the curse was nothing more than a comical memory.

* * * * *

REQUEST YOUR FREE BOOKS!

2 FREE NOVELS
PLUS 2 **FREE GIFTS!**

KIMANI™ ROMANCE

Love's ultimate destination!

A brand-new miniseries featuring fan-favorite authors!

THE HAMILTONS  *Laws of Love*

Family. Justice. Passion.

Ann Christopher	Pamela Yaye	Jacquelin Thomas

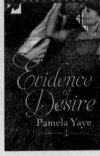

Available *September 2012*	*Available* *October 2012*	*Available* *November 2012*